# TIME

# WINDOWS

# TIME

# WINDOWS

## Kathryn Reiss

Harcourt Brace Jovanovich, Publishers
San Diego   New York   London

Library of Congress Cataloging-in-Publication Data
Reiss, Kathryn.
Time windows/Kathryn Reiss. — 1st ed.
p. cm.
Summary: Thirteen-year-old Miranda moves with her family to a
small Massachusetts town and a new house in which a mysterious
dollhouse allows her to see into the past, where she discovers her
new home exerts an evil influence on the women of each
generation of inhabitants — including Miranda's mother.
ISBN 0-15-288205-7
[1. Dollhouses — Fiction.   2. Space and time —
Fiction.   3. Moving, Household — Fiction.]   I. Title.
PZ7.R2776Ti   1991
[Fic] — dc20     90-22018

For
DOROTHY MOLNAR, my mother,
EDMUND REISS, my father,
and
TOM STRYCHACZ, my husband

Three who have long sustained me
with support, encouragement and love

And time yet for a hundred indecisions,
And for a hundred visions and revisions.
*— T. S. Eliot*
*From "The Love Song of J. Alfred Prufrock"*

# Ever After

Ever after, on muggy, magnolia-scented days, Miranda would stop whatever she was doing and stand silent for a minute or two. She was trying to remember.

Something special had happened once. Something wonderful and amazing. Something terrifying, too. Something absolutely impossible. But when she cast her mind back over all the events in her life up till now, she found nothing to account for this sharp certainty. Nothing was special in the way she knew *this* was.

The mystery tantalized her. When memory tickled, she'd stop her bike and stand in the road, tasting the hot summer air. And in her bedroom she'd stop playing her flute, staring instead at the old dollhouse in the corner by the windows. Strangest of all were the slips in conversation when she was with Dan. They'd be doing homework together, or walking to the bus stop, and she'd say: "Remember when—?" and then stop, with no idea at all what she had meant to say.

Threads of memory, like dreams, tried to weave themselves into a story. But—as with dreams—the harder she thought, face bent in a frown of concentration, the strands fluttered like spider gossamer, broke, and were gone.

# 1

Miranda's parents were singing Sinatra's old song "New York, New York" in the corniest way, trying to harmonize. Miranda tugged on her seat belt and twisted around to see out the rear window. The moving truck, which had been following their car steadily for the last hour, was now out of sight behind a curve in the highway. "Slow down! We've lost them!" she interrupted.

Her father halted in mid-yodel. "Don't worry. They know the way."

Miranda watched until the big truck lumbered into sight again, then leaned forward between the two front seats. "It's okay now."

Her parents launched into the last verse, raising their voices and grinning at each other. Miranda started laughing; they sounded so awful.

"Come on, Mandy," protested her mother when they'd finished. "You're supposed to be such a lover of music!"

"Well, that's just it, Mither. I love music so much, I

can't bear to listen anymore!" she kidded. Her parents were always doing this in the car — singing their hearts out without a care for staying in tune or knowing the right words. Miranda would make snide remarks, but usually she couldn't help humming along.

"Okay, then how about if you sing us something?" said her father. "In your perfect pitch. That'll give us a chance to rest up for the grand finale."

"To be sung as we drive into our new driveway," added her mother.

"Okay," agreed Miranda. " 'Home on the Range'?"

"Massachusetts doesn't have ranges," said her father. "How about something nice and sentimental, like 'Home Sweet Home'?"

"I don't know the words."

Both her parents screeched into song, her mother thumping the steering wheel to keep time:

> *"Be it e-ver so hum-ble,*
> *There's no-o place like home —"*

Miranda clapped her hands over her ears and pressed her face against the side window. But she was smiling.

The move from New York City to Garnet, Massachusetts, had not been Miranda's idea. She sulked when her parents first told her they would leave as soon as school was out for the summer. Miranda's mother, Helen Browne, was a doctor, and she had decided to open a private practice rather than stay on at the large New York hospital. "This is my chance," she told Miranda. "Garnet needs a new doctor, and I've wanted out of here for years." And Miranda's father, Philip Browne, who had taught history at the city college since long before Miranda was born, said the move would be a good change for him, too. "I'm just plain tired of teaching," he said.

"But, Dad!" Miranda protested. "Who's going to support us? You can't quit!"

"I quit smoking after twenty years. I can quit teaching after twenty years, too! Anyway, Mither's been earning a lot more than I have for a long time. I'll just take a year off and think about what I want to do next."

Helen laughed. "I'll try to support you in the style to which you've become accustomed, Miranda."

Philip glanced around their tiny, crowded apartment. "You'll be doing better than that without even trying. Just getting out of the city is going to make a big difference to me."

So it was settled. For Miranda, the worst part of moving was leaving her best friend, Nicole. But she stopped feeling sad almost as soon as their car left the New York City limits. Thirteen and a half years in New York City—Miranda's whole life—had left her with a keen appreciation for wide open spaces and fresh air. And both of these, Miranda could see as they left the city behind, would not be hard to find in Garnet. She wound down the window and gulped in the fragrant rush of wind.

Fresh air had as much to do with her parents' decision to move as her mother's new practice did, Miranda knew. Her father had been sick for the past two years—short of breath, overweight, with high blood pressure. He had dizzy spells and coughing fits that seemed to shake the walls of their apartment. But even when his doctor told him what Helen had said for years, that he'd die before he turned fifty if he didn't give up smoking and lose sixty pounds, Philip didn't listen. It wasn't until the day he keeled over while teaching his American History class at the college that he agreed they might be right. He smashed his head on a desk when he fell, and he had to have eighteen stitches and stay in bed for a week.

The rest gave him plenty of time to think. And when he got up again, he had a new determination.

"You two are the most important things in my life," he told Helen and Miranda. "I've been stupid. Things are going to change around here."

As always, he was a man of his word. He gave up smoking and joined a weight-loss program at the hospital where Helen worked. As Philip began to emerge from ill health a new man, his complaints about his work increased. "This teaching," he grumbled, "is a rat race. Packs of students every term — and are they listening? Does anything ever sink in? The frustration is what drove me to smoke and overeat in the first place, I'm telling you."

"Then get out, Phil," said Helen.

And so here they all were, getting out.

The road into Garnet wound past cornfields, an old cemetery, whitewashed barns and farmhouses, and so many trees that Miranda felt they were driving into a forest. The town itself was small and full of old-fashioned brick buildings, frame houses, and more trees. Outside the town the road narrowed and became a lane, and after about a mile Helen turned the car onto a side road that was paved in brick and wound up a hill. This was their new street, she told Miranda. There were only four houses on it—two at the bottom of the hill and two at the top. Theirs was at the top, across the street from what seemed to be a mansion. Both houses were surrounded by pine woods.

Philip awoke with a grunt as the car stopped—he had been dozing since they left the highway.

"Well!" said Helen. *Be it e-ver so hum-ble—"*

Miranda stared at the house in amazement. It was nothing like what she had imagined when her parents first described their new home. They had driven to Garnet one day while she was in school, spent a few hours with a real estate agent, and returned to the city jubilant at the great deal they'd stumbled upon. Philip had said the house was big, but he hadn't mentioned how it seemed to brood, looming among tangled weeds.

In the tradition of New England architecture, the house was of white clapboard, or of what had once been white clapboard but was now a tattered gray-white. Peeling paint flaked off the porch railings, and Miranda saw that a front window was smashed. Helen had told her there would be room enough for a vegetable garden, but she had not prepared Miranda for the expanse of flowering bushes, waist-high grass, and overgrown shrubs that created a fairy-tale nest in which the house squatted.

"Welcome home, ladies." Philip smiled. "What do you think, Mandy?"

Miranda jumped out of the car without answering and ran up the tangled path to the front door. She felt giddy with excitement.

Helen hurried up the walk behind her. "Oh my," she moaned. "It looks a lot more dilapidated now than it did last month."

Philip laughed, following on her heels with the door key dangling from one finger. "I've got my work cut out for me, I'll give you that. But that's good — it'll keep me off the streets."

Helen squeezed his arm. "City slicker turned handy-man!"

"You'd better believe it," he said. "I have big plans for this place." He turned the key in the lock.

"I know. But it looks so unlived-in." Helen stepped into the entrance hall.

"It *is* unlived-in," he said, right behind her. "But we're here to change all that."

"Oh, it's spooky!" cried Miranda, pushing past them. The hall was large and dim, and her voice echoed. She had not counted on the new place being much, but she could tell right away that her parents had found something special. It had to do with the atmosphere. A flash of intuition told her there was something here she'd missed out on in the city — maybe just the nooks and crannies for privacy. Maybe something else.

"Spooky only on the outside, Mandy," Philip responded. "The whole place will change once we get a few coats of paint on the walls and fix the shutters." He flicked a switch and the hall lights blazed, illuminating a carved oak stairway. "Well, at least the real estate agent is taking care of us. Last time we were here, the lights weren't working."

"Why not, Dad? Who lived here before?" Miranda stood in the middle of the hall feeling disoriented. She was half listening to her father's answer, half planning which of the several doors off the hallway to open first.

"I don't know the whole history of the house, but I do know the last family to live here moved out in the 1940s after the place caught fire. No one has lived here since."

Miranda opened the first door on the left, and they walked through a large dining room and into the kitchen, where the late afternoon sun shone orange through the milky glass of the back door. "No one has lived here in fifty years? Weird."

"It's a long time," agreed Helen, leaning up against the counter. She stood, silent, looking around the kitchen. "It sure is different from our kitchen in New York. Look at these old, beat-up cupboards. And all this floor space! I'll have to walk a mile just to prepare a meal."

"You'll be able to give up jogging, Helen. Just work out while you cook!"

"Where was the fire, Dad?" asked Miranda. "How did it start?"

"I don't know much about it," Philip said, running his hand over the dark tangles of Miranda's hair. "It was in the attic — and shortly afterward, the family living here moved back to Boston. I think that's what the agent said."

"Was anyone hurt?" Miranda asked.

"No — it only blackened a corner of the attic. Not much damage at all. You'll see."

"Yeah, but why hasn't anyone lived here since?"

"I'm not sure, Mandy," Philip responded.

Helen carried in a box and pulled out cups, a pan, instant coffee, canned milk, and spoons. She glanced over her shoulder at Philip. "Didn't the agent say that the last family to live here couldn't sell the house because of the terms of some will? They inherited it and had to pass it on to their children. But the children who finally inherited it weren't bound by the will and didn't have any qualms about selling the place. That's how we were able to get it."

Miranda walked around the room, looking in cupboards while her mother put the coffee water on to boil. The kitchen was easily as big as their living room in New York. She liked the high ceiling, the brick fireplace, the hugeness of the space. She tried to picture it after they all got busy with paint and window cleaner and hung bright curtains at the windows. She could see the three of them sitting at the table in this kitchen on Sunday mornings, reading the paper. She knew they would be happy here.

While her parents drank their coffee in the kitchen, Miranda wandered back through the pantry to explore the other rooms. Despite the fact that the house was unlived-in, it had a friendly, welcoming feeling. All the rooms had high ceilings. There were built-in cupboards in the dining room and built-in bookshelves on either side of the fireplace. Miranda stood in the center of each room and tried to imagine the space filled with their own furniture, china, and books. As in the kitchen, she could see her family living here happily. Good vibes, Nicole would say.

In the room at the back of the house Miranda stood before the bay window and looked out on the overgrown backyard. She decided she would stand in this window while she practiced her flute—once her father tamed the knee-high grass and planted flowers.

Miranda circled back into the hallway and found a tiny bathroom with a sharply sloping ceiling tucked under the stairs. She headed back into the front hall to climb the stairs to the bedrooms. But just as she was starting up, she glanced out the open front door and saw the moving truck lumbering into the driveway.

"Here come the movers," she called, running back into the kitchen.

"Right on time, too," said her father, setting down his mug. He unlocked the back door. Miranda followed him out into the overgrown garden. She fingered the shiny leaves on a vine tendril that draped itself over her shoulder as she watched the men lift their familiar furniture out of the truck and set it among the weeds.

"This your bed, honey?" The deep voice belonged to one of the two burly men who moved toward her, holding her bed aloft.

"Yes," she said. "But I haven't seen the bedrooms yet. I don't know where you should put it."

"Go ask, then, kiddo," said the other, shifting the heavy frame. "Think this is made of feathers?"

Miranda hurried over to her father, who was consulting with Helen and the driver of the van about the best way to move the long oak bookcases into the house. "Dad," interrupted Miranda. "Where is my bedroom?"

"Go pick one, Mandy. There are four—but Mither and I have already reserved the biggest one!"

Miranda raced back into the front hall and leaped up the stairs two at a time. She found herself in another large, square hall with five closed doors. The one directly ahead opened into a bathroom, where, under a small window, the bathtub squatted on great clawed feet. Back in the hall, she tried the other doors. The first opened into a huge square room with two built-in closets. Probably the master bedroom, already reserved. She closed the door and moved on. There was one large corner room and two smaller rooms. She chose the corner room because it had a window seat and a big tree outside the window. The remaining rooms, she knew, were to be her mother's and father's offices. In a house this size, Miranda wouldn't have to pick her way around the piles of important papers and books that had littered the tiny rooms of their New York apartment.

Miranda scrutinized her new bedroom. The walls were covered with a tattered wallpaper patterned with different models of old-fashioned airplanes. She narrowed her eyes and transformed the room: white paint on the walls, her blue tassled rug on the floor, new curtains at the wide windows. She imagined spending the winter reading in her window seat. It could be made very cozy with a bright cushion for the wooden bench.

She stepped into the hall again just as the two heavy-set movers appeared at the top of the stairs lugging her bed. "In here," she said, motioning them to set the bed along the wall next to the window seat.

Soon the house rang with voices as the Brownes directed the moving men and with the solid thuds of furniture being placed in its new home.

When the truck was unloaded and had driven down the hill, Helen and Philip moved wearily through the rooms, checking that everything had survived the journey intact. Miranda trailed behind, feeling the strangeness. "A stranger's house," she murmured. It smelled so different, so old, as if a lot of things had happened there. Living room, dining room, family room ("library," Philip called it), kitchen — all so much bigger than the apartment they'd just left. Their voices echoed off the bare walls and the furniture seemed to float in the great rooms.

"Once the carpets are unrolled and curtains hung at the windows, you won't hear the echoes anymore and the furniture will settle in," Helen assured Miranda. But Miranda shrugged off the reassurances. She *liked* the echoes.

They ate a picnic supper of cold sandwiches and fruit at the kitchen table. Then Helen and Philip started unpacking boxes. Miranda unpacked the blender and food processor, then headed up to her new room to arrange her books. At the top of the stairs, she stopped.

The attic. She had not seen the attic yet. She opened the narrow door and set one foot on the first step. At that moment the warm evening air grew unbearably dense. She couldn't breathe. Miranda jerked back into the hall, gasping. She gulped in the hallway air, which seemed breezy and fresh in comparison. She groped along the wall for the light switch, flicked it on, and stared up the long flight of narrow steps.

"Stale air," she muttered, starting up. A second door at the top stood slightly ajar, its latch hanging loosely, torn from the wood. Miranda reached the top and pushed that door open. The attic before her was large and dark. One corner was blackened. Charred fragments of ashy wallpaper littered the floor.

Cobwebs hung all around the room, draped across a few odds and ends of furniture that had been left by the previous owners. Old picture frames leaned in one corner. A child's school desk stood under the eaves. Long, low bookcases lined the wall beneath the windows. Miranda blew dust off one windowsill and struggled to raise the window. With creaks and scrapes and flying dust it jerked upward, letting the fresh evening air surge in like a cleansing shower. Now she saw, back in a far corner of the attic room, a large box—no, not a box...Gingerly Miranda stepped through the dust and cobwebs and examined the wooden structure. It was a dollhouse.

So tall it nearly reached Miranda's chest and about four feet wide, the house sat squarely in the dust-filled corner. It seemed vaguely familiar to Miranda and she walked around it, puzzled, trying to place it. She crouched down behind it and realized she was looking into a scale model of her new bedroom, window seat and all. Of course the dollhouse seemed familiar — it was a replica of her own new house, right down to the tiny bricks in the chimney and the molded front porch railings! Who had made it? Why hadn't they taken it away when they moved? The little empty rooms looked very much like the large ones Miranda had found when she walked into their house for the first time that afternoon.

Although the dollhouse walls were papered in unfamiliar patterns, the house was identical to the life-sized one. Miranda found it charming. She longed to see it in daylight; the single bulb lighting the attic by night was insufficient, and no moonlight shone in through the windows. The overhead bulb cast long shadows across the big, bare room, shrouding the dollhouse in darkness. Miranda raised herself onto her knees to look into the dollhouse attic. It, too, was dusty, dark, and bare, and on the dollhouse attic floor someone had written **WATER** in thick black crayon.

She raised her eyes and peered through the dollhouse attic windows out into the real attic. Across the room she saw a large dressmaker's dummy standing in one corner. She hadn't noticed that before; it looked like the one her grandmother kept in the sewing room to try on clothes as she made them on her sewing machine.

"Mandy!" Helen's voice floated up the attic stairs. "I thought you were unpacking!"

Miranda jumped up and ran to the top of the stairs. "Come up and see what I've found! There's a fantastic old dollhouse! And there's loads of old stuff, and a dressmaker's dummy like Grandma's—" She wheeled around, gesturing toward the windows as her mother and father started up the stairs. Then suddenly she stopped cold. The dressmaker's dummy was gone.

"What a lovely old dollhouse," exclaimed Helen with pleasure as she inspected the structure. "It's really a work of art. We'll have to bring it down and clean it up. You can keep it in your room, if you want. Or maybe it should go downstairs in the family room."

"The *library*," Philip teased.

Miranda forced herself to turn away from the empty corner where the dummy had stood only seconds before. She stared at her parents.

"You guys?"

"Hmm?" Helen knelt behind the dollhouse.

"I thought I saw a dressmaker's dummy over there. Like Grandma's."

Helen poked her head up and smiled quizzically at Miranda. "Where?"

"Right over there." She hesitated. "It *was* there. I, uh, at least I *thought* it was there." She pointed to the corner. "But now it isn't."

"No," agreed Philip. And Helen shrugged.

"You probably just saw shadows—they played a trick on you. It's really too dark up here to see much of anything." She ducked back behind the house. "But look at the tiny floorboards, Phil! They're amazing!"

Miranda moved to the stairs, suddenly feeling cold in the stuffy room. "I'm going down." She glanced back once to see if the dressmaker's dummy had reappeared.

It had not.

Hours later, her books unpacked and her clothes arranged in her dresser drawers, Miranda slid into her familiar bed in the new, unfamiliar bedroom. She sighed. It had been a long and tiring day. And it *was* dark in the attic, too dark to see properly.

She lay awake for a long time. The room was very quiet. The silence bothered her. She was used to traffic passing by the apartment all night: the sirens of ambulances, the clatter of trucks, the constant hum of cars whooshing by on the freeway. The stillness of the Garnet summer night hurt her ears. Then, in the bushes outside, a whole chorus of chirps and chortles began—crickets and tree frogs, her father had told her—and their songs disturbed her even more than the silence had. Tossing and turning, Miranda thought back over the events of the long day. One last thought echoed in her mind for a suspended moment before she drifted off to sleep: What happened to the dressmaker's dummy?

# 2

Miranda dreamed about biking around the new town and awoke with this plan in mind. Full of energy, she jumped out of bed, threw on a T-shirt and a faded pair of blue track shorts, and raced down the stairs. Exploring the neighborhood would be great here. Biking had not been much fun in the city because of all the traffic. As she sat down with her parents at the kitchen table, she imagined herself soaring along country lanes with the wind in her face.

"Have some cereal," said Philip, passing her the box. "Then we've got to get to work."

"Work!"

Helen raised her eyebrows. "You know, like pitching in and unloading the car and dusting and vacuuming and pulling weeds—"

"I get it, Mither." She spooned cereal into her mouth, her shoulders drooping considerably. Housework was the thing she hated most. But by the look in her parents' eyes this morning, she knew there would be no getting out of work today until everything was done. "Where do I start?"

Several hours later, Miranda sat back on her heels and brushed her dark hair off her forehead. She admired her new bedroom. All her clothes and books had found new places last night, but now the rest was settled in as well. Games in the bookcase — Clue and Monopoly and Trivial Pursuit. A chess set arranged on the window seat — her father was still promising to teach her to play. Her flute lay on the desk. Lambchop, her ragged stuffed lamb — a relic of babyhood — sat in his place of honor on her pillow. Miranda smiled at him, satisfied with her morning's work.

Helen poked her head into the room. "Good job, Mandy. It's a great room. I love the window seat. We'll have to go into town and look for a big cushion." Her arms were full of boxes. "Help me get the rest of this stuff?"

"What stuff?"

"Things I want put up in the attic — there's a pile in the hall."

Miranda came to see. "Mither, you are a pack rat!" She hoisted an old record player and a sleeping bag into her arms and staggered up to the attic after her mother.

Helen paused beside the windows, scraping away dirt with a fingernail. "Thanks. Just drop it all there. And would you run downstairs and ask Dad for some window cleaner and a pile of newspapers?"

"Newspapers?"

"Best thing for polishing glass. It doesn't leave streaks."

Miranda ran down the stairs again, returning with a bucket of ammonia water, some old rags, and the newspaper. They set to work scrubbing the window-panes.

"Does it seem all work and no play?" Helen asked sympathetically. "I know. But once we get this place cleaned up, it will really feel like home. You'll have time to meet the neighbors after lunch, I promise."

Miranda shined a window with crumpled newspaper. The windows looked out onto the large expanse of pine woods that bordered their property. The trees on that side were quite dense; she could barely see the house across the street through them.

While Miranda worked on the windows, Helen stacked boxes under the eaves. She brought up a broom and swept the cobwebs and dirt from the beams. Soon the large attic room grew lighter and less gloomy. It smelled fresher from the cleaning.

"I'll go down and make lunch," Helen said after a while. "Can you finish up here and come down in about ten minutes?"

"Sure. I'm starving." And then Miranda was alone in the attic.

She finished the last window quickly, then blew the heavy curls off her forehead. It was stuffy even with the windows open. She stood up and shuffled around the attic, stopping to straighten a pile of blankets in plastic bags, and then she wandered over to the doll-house.

In the light of day now streaming though the clear windows, she saw the little house was older than she had thought and some of the tiny porch railings were loose. She walked behind the house and knelt on the floor so she could see into the rooms. When she raised herself onto her knees, her eyes were just level with the dollhouse attic. She examined the black-crayoned writing on the floor. **WATER** . She puzzled over that for a moment. Then she peered out through the dollhouse attic windows into her own attic — at the suitcases now lined up under the eaves, the stack of lamp shades, the dressmaker's dummy . . .

The dressmaker's dummy!

Miranda jumped to her feet and stared over the roof of the house. *There was no dressmaker's dummy!* She sucked in her breath. It must be the heat in the attic. It was making her see things. But when she crouched down again and peered out into the big attic through the little windows, the dressmaker's dummy was standing there in the corner by the windows, next to a large, old-fashioned wooden trunk. She did not have to stand up and look over the house again to know that her family had brought no such trunk with them. She would have tripped over that trunk, if it had been there, when she stood in that same corner clean-ing the windows . . .

The windows. The windows she saw in the dress-maker's dummy's attic were dark. They were covered with black cloth. And the rags and crumpled newspaper and the bucket of ammonia water she'd left on the floor—where were they? The low bookcases beneath the windows—the ones she had just washed clean—were draped in cobwebs, their shelves filled with musty books and toys.

Miranda closed her eyes. "When I open my eyes," she thought desperately, "everything will be okay. Please, *please*, let everything be okay."

She opened her eyes and peered through the little windows again. And there in the big attic stood the dressmaker's dummy.

"Help," whispered Miranda. She suddenly felt afraid, too afraid to stand up and run out of the attic. No way could she cross the floor, walk past the dummy that shouldn't be there at all ... She sat back on her heels, eyes tightly shut again. "Please, please ..."

"Mandy!"

Her eyes flew open and she held her hands to her mouth, stifling a gasp.

"Mandy, lunch is ready!" Helen's voice wound up the stairs, reaching out to her as she cowered behind the old dollhouse.

"Mither?" Miranda's voice was unsteady. She stood up, ready now to run.

As she stepped away from the dollhouse, the room came back into focus. Normal. Okay. There were the clean windows. The stack of blankets. There were the rags and crumpled newspapers and the pail of ammonia water. Miranda stood poised for flight, and then she stopped. Was she crazy? She held her breath, ducked once more behind the dollhouse, and closed her eyes. "I dare you," she said aloud. "I *double* dare you!" Then she opened her eyes and stared out through the little windows. There were the dressmaker's dummy, the wooden trunk, the windows covered in black cloth. She stood up again. Normal!

"You've been a big help," said Helen. "Go on out for that bike ride. Maybe you'll meet the neighbors."

Somehow the neighborhood held less promise now. Miranda couldn't take her mind off the dollhouse up in the attic, waiting for her as she ate her sandwich.

"It's getting too hot up there," protested Helen.

But Miranda carried the fan upstairs and set it to work stirring the heavy air around. She wanted to be alone in the attic. She knelt at first in front of the house and looked through the windows into the tiny rooms. Nothing unusual there; just the inside of the house and, beyond it, the corner walls of her own life-sized attic room. Then she picked up some of the crumpled newspapers and stuffed them into the doll-house attic. She knelt in front of the house again and looked in through the little windows. Okay, nothing weird there; the balls of paper lay in the dollhouse exactly where she'd put them.

But now for the real test. She removed the papers from the house and arranged them carefully on the floor about three feet from the front of the structure. Then she stationed herself behind the house and low-ered herself onto her knees. "It was only the heat be-fore," she assured herself, resting her arms on the dollhouse attic floor and peering out through the tiny windows at the spot on the floor where she had put the balls of crumpled paper.

She drew back with a sharp exclamation of horror. Instead of the wads of paper, a little girl stood in front of the dollhouse, bouncing a red-and-blue ball and trying to hit it with a small wooden bat. Miranda flung herself backward, her heart pounding. A wave of terror washed over her and pulled at her stomach like a salty undertow.

*I'm going to die!* screamed a voice in Miranda's head. Was that her voice? The terror was pure, unadulterated. She wrenched her eyes away from the dollhouse windows, and her own attic swam once again before her eyes. She rose shakily to her feet. The wads of paper were in front of the little house just where she had placed them.

Miranda was sweating, but her mouth felt parched. She kicked the paper across the floor. It was true! Somehow, it was true. When she looked outward through the little windows of the dollhouse attic, her own attic disappeared. The place she saw was another place, a different attic. Even with her back to the little house now, she could feel it there. She felt compelled to turn back to the dollhouse, to walk behind it. The terror was still churning in her stomach, but it was milder now. She forced it down and rested her elbows again on the ledge of the dollhouse attic. She looked out through its tiny windows.

In the big attic the little girl tossed the ball into the air and lunged after it with the bat. She appeared to be seven or eight years old, and she wore a striped blue dress with long puffed sleeves and a starched blue sash tied in an oversized bow at the back. Her long blonde hair was pulled into two pert braids tied at the ends with blue ribbons. On her feet she wore shiny black shoes that covered her ankles and were fastened with a long row of tiny black buttons. Miranda drank in all these small details with the same sudden thirst with which she'd taken in the details of the room beyond. The terror was gone now. In its place Miranda felt a need to see everything.

The walls were bright with whitewash. The low bookcases lining the walls under the windows were also white and filled with toys. The little girl swatted at the ball, and this time she managed to hit it with her bat — *thwap!* — and went running after it, squealing with laughter.

Miranda found herself smiling and standing up to go over to the girl, her lips forming the question: "Who are you?"

But her question fell on an empty attic. As soon as she stood up, she was alone in the attic once again. And the attic was her own.

She crouched again, but when she looked back out through the little windows the child was gone. And the attic she saw was dim and dusty. The dressmaker's dummy stood sentry in the far corner under the eaves, draped in cobwebs. The low bookcases were filled with the child's toys, but now they were grimy and mildewed. Miranda recognized the ball and bat on the top shelf. Outside the tiny attic windows, it was raining. Miranda listened to the pattering drops for a moment, then cautiously peeked around the side of the house. The day outside *her* newly scrubbed attic windows gleamed fresh and bright in the summer sun. She focused back through the dollhouse.

Through its little windows she could see the larger windows of a different attic—another one? She could see rain pelting the glass, droplets running in rivulets down the panes. Where was the little girl? How many attics could there be?

Someone was climbing up the attic stairs. Miranda heard the footsteps and watched as the knob on the stairway door turned. Left. Right. Then she heard a piping voice. "Mommy, it's locked."

She didn't need to glance over the top of the dollhouse to know that the attic door in *her* attic stood open. And the latch was broken. The doorknob rattled. Someone on the other side coughed. "There's no key," said a woman's voice, not Miranda's mother's. "Run down and tell Daddy to bring up a crowbar."

"Will we have to break down the door? Will we, Mommy?" asked a child's excited voice.

"No, Timmy. Just the lock."

More footsteps on the stairs, and a man's low voice. Then banging, and the scrape of metal. Miranda pressed her hands down on the dollhouse attic floor. They were going to break in! Whoever they were, they would be in the attic in another minute.

The door flew open and two little boys about four and five years old tumbled into the room, followed by a slender, gentle-looking woman with soft brown hair waved around her face and a tall, thin man with black hair. Miranda stared in astonishment, but these ghosts—if that's what they were—induced no terror at all.

"Look, Mommy!" called the younger boy as he raced around the room. "What a mess!"

"I'll bet there are loads of spiders and stuff," called the other boy, beaming a large flashlight into the corners.

"Ugh, what filth!" said the woman. "Don't touch anything, boys." She looked around with distaste, then turned to the man. "This looks like it was a playroom once. I can't imagine why it was left locked up. Can you?"

He shook his head. "No, but I'm beginning to think old Uncle Sigmund was pretty eccentric. His lawyer said he locked the place up and just left everything to rot, and he wouldn't even hear of selling anything or letting anyone else move in."

"It's sad," she murmured. "He must have really become disturbed after his wife and child died."

"Apparently he never got over it. Just became a recluse—lived all alone in a rooming house in Boston. Even my own mother didn't see him for years, and she had always been his favorite sister. I can't imagine why he decided to leave the house to me in his will."

"Probably because you're his favorite sister's son!" she said, crossing to the windows. "It's so lucky for us! Look at the garden—all that space! Such a perfect place for the boys."

He looked out over her shoulder. "Lots of room for that vegetable garden you've always wanted."

"True—but we've got to make the house habitable first." She turned back to survey the room. "Imagine letting everything just decay!"

"Can this be our playroom, Mommy? There are lots of funny toys!" The older boy held up a tin figure. "What does this do?"

The man crossed the room to him. "It's an old penny bank!" he exclaimed. "An organ grinder with a monkey. They were popular when I was a boy."

The smaller boy was still rummaging through the shelves. "Look at this!" he crowed, holding up the dusty bat and the red-and-blue ball. "Can we play with this stuff?"

"Yes, Timmy," said his mother. "But we have to take it down and wash it first." She looked at the man. "What about these windows? Do you think light might shine out them from the hallway downstairs?"

"Probably not. Not if we close the doors at the top and bottom of the stairs."

She hesitated. "Well—I've got a lot of cloth. Maybe I should make up some curtains. Just to be safe."

"How come we have to have black curtains all over the place?" asked Timmy. "They're so ugly!"

"There's a war on, stupid!" answered his brother scornfully.

"No name calling, Jeff," warned their father. "Timmy, when the windows are dark at night, then any planes flying overhead won't see the lights from houses. They won't know there's a town down here and won't bother dropping any bombs. The planes fly at night so we won't see them, and we want to make sure they can't see us, either."

Timmy's voice quavered. "But why do people want to drop bombs on us?"

"Because they're the enemy, dopeface!" said Jeff. "Enemies always try to kill everybody!"

"I said, no name calling," repeated the man.

"But why is there a war?" Timmy persisted.

"Boys, come look at this big dollhouse," said the woman. Miranda cringed as she saw them coming. They came closer and closer until she could see the chocolate ice cream stain on the smaller one's shirt. The older boy stood on tiptoe to look in the attic windows, and suddenly his brown eyes were centimeters away from Miranda's own. She froze, petrified. She could see the freckles across the bridge of his nose, but he didn't seem to see her at all.

"Hey, look!" he called to his father. "It's just like our house, only little!"

He disappeared suddenly from Miranda's range of vision.

"Let's see the inside," said the woman. Miranda watched as the woman's skirt moved outside the attic windows. When the skirt disappeared, Miranda caught her breath. They must have gone behind the house — must be standing right where she was kneeling, looking right down at her . . .

Trembling, Miranda raised her eyes — and saw no one.

When she looked back through the little attic windows, the real attic was empty and the windows were covered by black curtains. "I missed it," she said to herself. "They made the curtains and hung them up and went away in just the second it took me to look up!" She leaned back against the wall and closed her eyes. The energy that had held her to the dollhouse windows, kept her an avid observer, was gone. She felt drained.

"Honey, what are you doing?"

Miranda leaped to her feet and stared over the house. Helen walked across the attic, picking up the paper balls and the pail of ammonia water. "My, you're jumpy."

"I—I was just . . . thinking."

"Daydreaming," said her mother. "You've been up here all afternoon! Dad and I are going for a walk— try to rustle up some neighbors around here. I'm not used to things being so quiet. Come with us?"

"Mither?"

"Hmm?"

"Come here for a second. Look through these windows. Okay? Tell me what you see."

Helen crowded back into the corner obligingly. "Look through which window? Oh—well, I see the attic, of course."

Miranda walked around to stand in front of the house. "And can you see me now?"

Helen's face peered curiously through the windows. "Of course I can see you! Is something wrong, Mandy?"

Miranda crossed her arms, suddenly chilled in the

stuffy attic. "I just wondered..." Her voice trailed away, and she shrugged. She followed her mother toward the stairs, turning around once to look back at the dollhouse.

Its blank windows seemed to wink back at her.

# 3

By the end of their first week in the new house, their mail started arriving. Miranda had two letters from Nicole, who claimed to be miserable without her. Helen began moving things into her new office in the center of town and spent afternoons interviewing nurses and receptionists. The weather stayed muggy, and Philip usually emerged from the overgrown garden at dinnertime, dripping wet and covered with scratches from the briars. Miranda stayed inside, finding her large corner room cooler than the front porch during the day. She helped her mother sew a cover for the large pillow they'd purchased as a cushion for her window seat. After that, she sat in her window seat for hours at a time, staring out at the magnolia tree and, through its leaves, the roof of the big house across the road. She wasn't really seeing them, though. She was thinking about the dollhouse.

From time to time her parents would peek into the room and urge her to get busy doing something, but they didn't pester her much; they both thought she needed time alone to get used to the new house and the move.

"The family across the street has two boys," Helen informed Miranda. "I think one of them's your age. But they're all on vacation now." Miranda tried to look interested. She knew she should be interested. In New York she would have been.

Her parents went on long bike rides around town and on walks to explore the woods across the road from their house. They always asked Miranda to come with them, but she simply didn't want to go. She was running out of excuses: She'd told them she needed to stay inside to get used to the new house. She'd said she enjoyed the peace and quiet after the noise of New York.

All this was true, but there was more, and this was what she did not tell them. Her growing interest in the dollhouse had become almost an obsession—feeling the way she imagined her father's former cigarette addiction must have felt. She needed her "fix" at least once a day. The nicotine might stain her father's fingers and burn his throat, but he didn't care as long as he could pull that soothing, dangerous smoke into his lungs and relax. The dollhouse frightened her, but Miranda didn't care as long as she could lean into its little rooms and lose herself in its mysteries of the past.

While her parents were out meeting new neighbors and exploring Garnet's narrow side streets, Miranda would mount the steps to the attic and settle herself behind the dollhouse. She was learning how the magic worked.

In the different attics she could see through the little windows, the weather varied. And the seasons. Sometimes the windows in the attics she saw were bright and clean, and other times they were dull and grimy or covered with the black curtains. The attic the little girl played in had clean windows. The attic with the dirty windows seemed to be the same playroom—abandoned and older. The attic the family had broken into had black curtains now, but no one ever came up there. Miranda wondered if she had found a time machine. But she knew it couldn't be, because she only *watched* through the windows; she did not travel anywhere. She had to laugh at herself for feeling disappointed. *Idiot! Things like that don't happen in real life.*

But what *was* happening, she couldn't say.

When she looked through the windows of the dollhouse kitchen, she could see into the kitchen of her own house as it had looked in other times. And not only the kitchen windows possessed this magic; she could monitor every part of their house by moving around to peer out of different little windows. When she settled herself in the corner behind the dollhouse and rested her arms on the dollhouse attic floor, she had only to keep her eyes trained through its windows, and the whole house's past became her present.

Because she sometimes had to wait quite a while for anything to happen, she made the corner behind the house cozy with red cushions to sit or kneel on, a box of cookies, and even a book—so she could read while she waited for the house's occupants to return. She had borrowed the cushions from an old couch her father had put in the ancient stable they used as a garage, and she hoped her parents wouldn't notice. She had a strong sense that the dollhouse must be kept private. It would reveal its secrets to her, but it didn't want outsiders around.

The people she watched seemed quite real, almost familiar. They were at home in the house, as if they belonged there as much as she did. As if they, too, lived in the house. They went about their fairly normal lives, doing chores, having conversations. Everything they did, no matter how ordinary, fascinated Miranda.

Although the little girl's time did not appear often, Miranda learned—from hearing the name yelled angrily up the attic steps to the playroom—that the child was named Dorothy. Usually Miranda found Dorothy only in the playroom, although she searched for the child in all the other rooms. Once little Dorothy was being bathed in the big claw-footed bathtub when Miranda peered into the bathroom. A friendly-looking uniformed maid held the wriggling child tightly and laughed. "No squirming away from me this time, Miss Dorothy Arabella! Those golden locks are in dire need of a good wash!"

"No, Hannah! You'll get soap in my eyes!"

The other people in the house, the people Miranda had seen break into the attic, were relative newcomers to Garnet. The tall, thin man was named Andrew Kramer. He had inherited the old house from a recluse uncle and brought his wife, Iris, and their two sons, Timmy and Jeff, to Garnet from Boston. Andrew took the train to Boston every morning and did not return home until dark. Iris took care of the two little boys. She was a gentle, quiet woman, and Miranda felt drawn to her.

The problem with the dollhouse magic was that the time sequences were not chronological. Time didn't seem to have any proper order at all. One minute Miranda could be watching Jeff and Timmy build a castle out of blocks, and the next minute could find her peeking through the same windows at little Dorothy swinging her bat at the red-and-blue ball. It happened more than once already that Miranda would be listening to an exciting conversation between Iris and Andrew, only to have them leave the room. She would rush to the next little room to look out those windows, trying to follow them through the house. But if she did manage to find them again, they would be having a totally different conversation on another day—perhaps a month after the first conversation, perhaps a month before. And yet at other times the sequence moved logically, and Miranda was able to follow the family from room to room, never losing the drift of things.

On a Sunday morning during their second week in the new house, Helen and Philip went for a bike ride. Miranda begged off with the excuse that her nose was stuffy and she thought she had allergies. Her father raised his eyebrows, and her mother lowered hers in a frown.

"It's probably house dust up your nose," Helen said. "What you need is fresh air."

"I'll go out this afternoon. Promise!"

"We'll hold you to it, Mandy," said Philip. And then they were out the door, and Miranda was clattering up to the attic to see what the dollhouse people were doing.

She settled herself on the cushions, adjusted the fan, and gazed out through the kitchen window. No one was in the room, but it was not the Kramers' brightly painted kitchen Miranda had come to know. This was an older kitchen without a refrigerator, and a pump stood in one corner near a funny wooden sink. The smell of fresh hot bread hung in the air, and through the small window in the back door Miranda could see flakes of snow drifting lazily.

She looked around the room with interest, taking in the old-fashioned telephone hanging on the wall and the red-checked oilcloth covering the table. The orange glow from a fat black iron stove reflected warmly off the whitewashed walls and the polished oak floorboards. Finally she noticed a calendar on the far wall: January 1904.

January 1904! The reality of the time difference hit Miranda full force. While watching Iris and Andrew, she hadn't thought about it much. They wore the styles she'd seen in movies set during World War II, and once she heard Iris complaining to a neighbor lady about sugar rationing, but Miranda had never pinned the family down to a specific year.

Yet here it was. January 1904, and not Iris's kitchen. The same kitchen, yet perhaps another generation earlier. She felt the trickle of perspiration under her arms even as she stared at snowflakes outside the kitchen window. From somewhere in the house Miranda heard piano music, tinny sounding. At the back door window a face appeared in the frosty pane, and the door chimes rang, clear and melodic. The piano stopped and the dining room door swung open. A woman swept in on a wave of magnolia perfume, and Miranda's heart leaped in her throat. Terror poured into her stomach. She was going to be sick. She was going to die. *Helpmehelpmehelpmehelpme!* a voice screamed in her head.

She gripped the sides of the dollhouse and willed herself not to throw up and not to turn away. She knew if she did, she could lose this scene forever — and somehow she knew she must see it. This was important. She fought back the panic and whispered urgently to herself: *It's all right, it's all right, it's all right.*

The panic throbbed dully in the pit of her stomach. Miranda moved closer to the little kitchen windows. She had never seen anyone so beautiful in her life. The woman was tall and willowy, with a face like those on Greek statues: a straight nose, a noble mouth, regal eyes. She wore a deep violet dress, with black lace frothing across her bosom and fringing her wrists. The long skirt swished across the floor as she walked to the door. Her auburn hair rose high, piled and twisted elaborately. She answered the door.

A man dressed in gray entered the kitchen, brushing snow off his shoulder and beard. "Lucinda, beloved!" He pulled off his gloves, tossing them onto the checkered oilcloth. He reached out to embrace her, but she held him at arm's length.

"You're wet, Donald. And cold." Her voice was low, husky. She took him by the hand and led him to a kitchen chair. "Wait here. I'll only be a moment." She swept from the room.

Donald tapped his fingers restlessly and removed his scarf. He opened his overcoat and fumbled inside his suit pocket, bringing out a watch on a gold chain. He looked at the watch, shook it, looked at it again and, frowning, replaced it. The smell of something burning wafted through the room.

Lucinda whirled back into the kitchen wrapped in a long fur cloak. "Oh, the bread! I forgot—" She reached for a towel and, covering her hand, opened the oven door. Smoke billowed out in a thick blanket. "Damnation!" She shrugged off her cloak, dropping it unceremoniously onto a chair. Miranda heard a tiny *ping* as if something had fallen out of the pocket. But no, nothing lay on the floor; it must have been the clink of the metal tongs against the oven as Lucinda drew out the charred loaves.

"Ruined." She flipped the bread into the sink and glared at the stove. "You black monster!"

"My dear, calm yourself. It doesn't matter." Donald hovered at her side and checked his watch again.

"Of all the rotten luck." Lucinda scowled. "I'll *never* learn to cook. Stupid Hannah! Why did she have to quit today of all days?"

Donald laughed, handing her the fur. "Darling Lucinda. A housewife you aren't! But where we're going, you won't need to be. You'll have everything I can give you! Ah, you don't know how much it means to me that we can finally get away. It's what I've always dreamed of." He embraced her and nuzzled her cheek.

She smiled at him. "Let's leave, then. We don't want to miss the train."

"But what about the kid? Where's Dorothy?"

"Mandy? We're home! What are you doing up there?"

At the sound of Philip's voice, Miranda tore her eyes away from the kitchen scene. "Coming!" she called. She peeked back into the kitchen for one last look. But instead of the beautiful Lucinda and handsome Donald in their traveling outfits, Iris and Andrew lounged at the table in their bathrobes, the early morning sun pouring in through the small window in the back door. They drank coffee from flowered china cups. Swing music with a strong downbeat resounded loudly from another room.

"I just don't like this house anymore," Iris was saying. "That's all there is to it. I hate it here!"

"There you go again," muttered Andrew. He sounded exasperated. "I'm sick of it. Can't you give me a rational explanation, for once?" He poured his coffee into the sink. "This stuff is terrible. I'm going to get dressed." He stomped out of the kitchen, shouting, "You kids turn off that radio! How many times have I told you not to touch it?"

Iris sighed and rested her head in her hands for a moment. Then she went to the sink and rinsed her cup. "I can't stand much more of this," she said softly.

At lunch Helen and Philip were full of news. "We've met the people across the road at last," Helen said. "The ones in that beautiful house. It's the oldest one in town, and they've turned it into the Garnet Museum. We've been invited over for dessert tonight."

"Mmm," murmured Miranda. She was hardly listening, thinking instead about Lucinda and Donald and wondering what was wrong with Iris.

"Earth to Mandy," said Philip.

"What?"

"You're really off in a world of your own these days, honey," he said. "What have you been up to?"

"Nothing, really." She didn't know why she felt she had to keep the dollhouse magic a secret—usually she told her parents everything. Somehow she felt this was different. "I—I just have a stomachache."

Helen leaned forward with concern in her eyes. "I thought it was your sinuses. Honey, are you coming down with something?"

"Maybe you should go lie down," added Philip. "You've hardly eaten anything."

"We can cancel dessert with the Hootons," added Helen.

"No, it's okay." The last thing she wanted was for them to be making a huge fuss over her. "I'll be fine in a while. I'll just rest for a half hour." Miranda left the room quickly and was up the stairs in seconds. She sat on her bed for a moment, fully intending to lie down for the promised half hour. But then she felt the attic irresistibly pulling her back.

She tiptoed quietly to the attic door and hurried up the steps. She walked toward the dollhouse, her eyes fixed on its little windows. The dollhouse, with its dark windows, its shuttered eyes looking into another world. The dollhouse, with its intricate carving, tiny hinges, miniature bricks and boards, and secrets.

The dollhouse. She slipped into place behind it.

Timmy lay across his bed in a small heap. His sobs, muffled by the thick blanket, were barely audible. The curtains were drawn against the patter of rain outside, but occasional flashes of lightning shot brilliant streaks across the wall.

Outside in the hall Timmy and Miranda heard the sound of voices, his parents' voices rising and falling in heated consultation. The door handle turned, clicked, turned the other way. Timmy's sobs rose painfully. "Timmy? Timmy! Open the door, son." That was Andrew's quiet voice.

"Timothy!" Iris sounded furious.

Timmy cried harder. "Go away," he screamed. "I hate you!"

"You open this door right now, young man,"

snarled Iris. "Open it now, or I'll take it off the hinges, and if I have to do that, you are going to get—"

"Now, Iris—," interjected Andrew. "Don't threaten him—"

"Timothy, I'm warning you. This is the last time I'm going to say it. *Open this door.*"

Timmy shuffled to the door, turned the key, and quickly flung himself back onto the bed. Iris burst into the room, her eyes glittering coldly. Andrew pushed past her and rushed to his son, gathering the small boy in his arms. "Hush, old boy. Hush now, it's all right." Timmy struggled in his father's arms for a second, then relaxed and lifted his tear-stained face.

"She *hurt* me, Daddy," he whimpered. "Why did she hurt me?"

Andrew's lips tightened and he threw an accusing look at his wife. Iris's face had grown pale. The hand she reached out to Timmy shook slightly.

"Can you tell me about it, Tim? Tell me what happened."

"She hit me," began Timmy softly, glancing timidly over his shoulder at Iris. "With a lamp. It—broke. And then she said I broke it. But I didn't, honest! She broke it herself, trying to catch me and Jeff. We were playing tag. She threw it at me . . ." His voice dwindled and he buried his face against Andrew's shoulder.

"Iris?" Andrew's voice was hollow.

Iris flinched, then moved closer to the bed. "Timmy, Timmy, baby, I'm sorry." Her voice shook and tears streamed down her face. "I don't know what came over me. I really don't know why I did it—I just had such a horrible headache all of a sudden...Oh, darling, please forgive me. I'm so sorry..."

"Don't cry, Mommy, don't cry," sobbed Timmy.

Her soft voice rose in near hysteria. "I don't even remember what happened! I can't remember!" She grabbed her husband's arm imploringly. "Please forgive me, Andrew, please."

Andrew lay back against the headboard, staring at her incredulously. "You hit him with a *lamp?* With a lamp—and you can't remember?"

"No," she moaned. "Oh, Andrew, please. I'm so afraid."

"God, Iris, you expect me to believe that?"

Iris wrapped her arms tightly around Timmy and smoothed his hair with her chin. "Andrew," she said. "It's the house. We've got to get out of this house ... I'm afraid here." Her hands trembled around the child.

"Afraid of what?" cried Timmy, lifting his head.

"Ssh, shush now," said Andrew, hastily standing up. "We should get some sleep and wake up fresh tomorrow. How about it, old boy?" He settled Timmy in bed, drawing up the covers. "We'd better go see where Jeff has gone off to," murmured Andrew, putting his arm around Iris's shoulders.

Iris stepped free and bent over Timmy again, gathering him into her arms. "Please believe I never meant to hurt you, Timmy," she whispered. "Please believe that."

Iris and Andrew moved to the door and Andrew reached out to flick off the light. Timmy's voice stopped his hand in midair. "Will you be here when I wake up?"

They looked at Timmy's reddened, tearful eyes and moved closer together. For a moment, Miranda was reminded of a seventeenth-century painting she once saw in the New York Art Museum: grieving parents standing over their dead child, a priest hovering near a window in the background, having arrived too late.

"Yes, darling, we'll be here. Always."

Miranda's stomachache was no lie now. She left the attic and went down to her room. She lay on her bed and covered her stomach with her palms.

Helen poked her head in. "What is it, Mandy?" She came in, followed by Philip. They stood by her bed.

"Okay, honey?" asked Philip.

Miranda lay on top of the sheet and looked at them leaning over her, watching her anxiously. For a second the scene appeared in her mind's eye as it would if she were watching it through the dollhouse windows. "It's just a stomachache," she told them. "Why are you looking at me like that?"

Philip stretched out his hand as if to feel her forehead for a fever but lowered it to stroke Miranda's face, cupping her chin. Helen leaned down and kissed Miranda's cheek.

A feeling of déjà vu stole over Miranda. Had this all happened before? She was suddenly no longer sure if she was the observer or if she was the one being observed. Was there another dollhouse in another time? Was someone looking into *her* bedroom, watching *her* parents bend over her in concern? Was someone else, in fact, reminded of a seventeenth-century oil painting? The soft cotton sheet felt scratchy against her cheek when she turned her head to the wall.

"Have a good nap, Mandy," said Helen.

The words seemed to fall from her lips, unbidden: "Will you be here when I wake up?" She stared at the wall. She could hear the surprise in their voices.

"Of course we'll be here," her mother said.

And her father added: "Always."

# 4

No breeze stirred the humid air that evening when Helen, Philip, and Miranda joined the Hooton family on the veranda of the huge old house across the street. Ed Hooton, a tall man with a red beard, welcomed them with a big smile and a tray of lemonade. Virginia Hooton shook hands all around and invited them to sit down in the wicker rockers that dotted the big porch. "I'm so glad you could come," she said. "And it's nice to meet you at last, Miranda. The boys'll be glad, too. There aren't any other young people on the street."

Miranda smiled at her and settled back into a rocker. She wasn't really interested in meeting "the boys"—although she did wonder a little at her own reaction. Back in New York she and Nicole both had had their eyes on the cute twins in algebra—Josh and Jon Allen—and finally were bold enough to ask them to the spring dance. They double dated. The guys sat on the bleachers most of the time, talking about basketball, while she and Nicole watched the dancers and wondered what they'd seen in the twins in the first place.

Before she'd moved, Miranda was already looking around for other possibilities. But here in Garnet boys — any other people, really — seemed less like possibilities and more like liabilities. She smiled at the realization that the little Kramer kids — or the beautiful Lucinda — were a lot more interesting than Josh Allen. Any of the dollhouse people were, for that matter.

Two boys bounded up onto the porch from the yard. The younger one was about Dorothy's age, Miranda guessed. The older was about her own age. Both had straight dark hair like their mother and almost identical faces.

"Hi," said the older boy. "I'm Dan. My parents have gone on for days about the new neighbors. But I was beginning to wonder whether you really existed."

"My name's Buddy," the younger boy said. "And you're skinny."

Miranda just looked at them. She had to reach inside herself to pull out her company manners and her usually sociable self. It seemed so long since she'd talked to anyone. She had grown so accustomed in the past weeks to just listening. She smiled at the boys with effort. "You guys look like twins, do you know that? Except in height, of course."

"And brains," said Dan.

The younger boy punched him in the arm. "You — "

"What grade will you be in?" Dan asked Miranda quickly.

"Eighth."

"I'll be in ninth. What classes are you going to take?"

Miranda hadn't registered at the new school yet; and when she admitted this, the talk on the porch turned to all the details of settling in that still needed to be handled.

"We're always amazed how quickly people settle into a new place," said Mrs. Hooton with a little laugh.

"I don't think I'd know the first thing about moving," added Mr. Hooton. "I've only lived away from Garnet for four years — and that was back in college. Of course, we travel on vacation, but that's different." His cigarette flared in the growing darkness. "Hootons out of Garnet are like fish out of water."

"Dad! You're supposed to quit smoking!" Buddy frowned at him.

"I'm not doing too badly, Buddy. Down to two a day."

"I gave up smoking this past year," said Philip. "It's hard to do, but worth it." He took a big, deep breath. "Just listen to those clean lungs! Not a rattle."

"Don't get Phil started," laughed Helen. "He's a walking advertisement for good health these days." She turned to Mrs. Hooton, changing the subject. "Have you lived here a long time, too?"

"Practically forever. My great-great-grandparents had a house down by the river."

"We think it's fitting that we should run the museum," said Mr. Hooton, "since our families are more or less museum pieces themselves."

The adults laughed and settled back with more lemonade, talking about the ups and downs of living in a museum. Mr. Hooton explained that he and his wife had both worked in a museum in Boston but had found the commute too tiring. "Then it dawned on us a couple of years ago that we were practically living in a museum already—with all the odds and ends and furniture and stuff we'd collected from our families through the generations. We thought, why not make all this history available to other Garnet families?"

"I admire your courage in taking a new track," said Philip, and went on to tell about leaving his teaching position. Dan and Buddy jostled each other's rocking chairs, each trying to rock faster and harder than the other. Miranda tucked her legs up under her and leaned her head back against the cushion in her chair. She stared out over the lawn, through the trees and across the street to where her own house crouched in the darkness. Fireflies glittered in the bushes around the porch. She closed her eyes, pictured the dollhouse, and felt a restlessness come over her. She wanted to be home.

"Hey, I said, want to toss a ball around?"

She opened her eyes and blinked at Dan. "Sorry, I didn't hear you."

"Were you asleep?" asked Buddy.

"No, I'm just tired." She smiled and shook her head. "I don't really want to play ball. You guys go ahead. I'm fine here." She picked her glass up off the table and sipped the lemonade.

"Oh, come on. I'll pitch nice and easy."

"Pitch as hard as you like. I'll have you know I played softball on my school team in New York!"

"Great! Then come on."

"No, really." She shifted in her chair and stared out over the lawn. "I don't feel like it now."

Dan shrugged. "Okay." He was off the porch in an instant, running out into the yard with Buddy. Miranda pretended to listen to the adults' conversation, counting fireflies in the dark until it was time to leave.

In the morning Helen drove their small car down the hill into town. Miranda sat in the front seat next to her, one arm around her flute case in her lap, the other resting on the window to catch the fresh, fragrant wind

"Ah, Mandy," said Helen. "What a great change from New York!"

Miranda had to agree. Garnet in summer was sparkling and scented with flowers from gardens bordering the shady yards of old and gracious houses set well back from the narrow streets. New York City in summer was gritty, oppressive, and smoggy, and the sidewalks radiated dust. Last year they'd had a heat inversion that lasted so long—the smog lying thick and heavy, obscuring the tops of skyscrapers—that there had been talk of gas masks. Miranda had had a doomed feeling that she would smother if the air-conditioning in the apartment broke down, as it sometimes did in the hottest weather. But here in Garnet a gas mask would be laughable, as ridiculous as a Halloween mask in July.

Helen drove leisurely through the quiet streets. "There's the village commons," she said. "Ed Hooton said the American troops practiced there during the

Revolutionary War." The commons stretched out before them on the left, a green, tree-filled park.
Children played on swings and slides while adults relaxed on blankets and read. The park benches, where
newspaper-reading citizens enjoyed their coffee
breaks, were surrounded by pigeons who demanded
and received donut crumbs and other tidbits.

"Here's our agenda," said Helen. "First we go to the
junior high and get you enrolled. Eighth grade already! I can't believe it."

Miranda grinned. Her mother said that sort of thing
every year.

"Then we'll look at wallpaper. And then we'll go to
see about your flute lesson. Virginia Hooton raved
about the woman. You'll have to do a little audition,
but don't worry. After that I have to go to my office to
interview the last nurse. Maybe you'd like to wait at
the library while I'm there — Virginia said it's all within
a minute's walk. Nice, isn't it, in a small town? Everything accessible — not like New York. My God! The
hours I've spent on subways just trying to get from the
hospital to the grocery store to the apartment!"

Miranda listened agreeably, watching the scenery.
Children roller-skated on the sidewalks. Bicycles
whizzed past. "Think of it!" exclaimed Helen. "You'll
be able to ride your bike to school!" Teenagers rode
tractor-sized lawnmowers around their front lawns,
creating geometric patterns in the grass.

Helen turned the corner onto Garnet's main street.
An ornate plaque hung by a heavy chain from a white
post in front of the Town Hall:

GARNET, MASSACHUSETTS

\* est. 1691 \*

A BIRD SANCTUARY

They turned another corner and pulled up beside Miranda's new school.

The school looked older than her New York school, but not as dirty. It was red brick with white trim, and there was another sign on a white post: GARNET TOWNSHIP JUNIOR HIGH SCHOOL.

"Oh, a city girl," exclaimed the principal with a smile. "Hope you're happy here, Miranda." They were in and out in no time, and Miranda settled back into the car seat, clutching a booklet titled "Rules and Regulations for Students," her new course schedule, and a slip of paper with her gym and hall locker combinations written down.

Helen stopped the car in front of a small house on a shady side street. "Sixteen Elm Street. This is it," she said. "Don't forget your flute!"

An elderly woman opened the front door as they came up the walk. "Hello!" she called to them in a high, quavery voice. "You must be the Brownes. I'm Eleanor Wainwright. Please come right in."

Miranda and Helen climbed the steps to the small front porch and followed Mrs. Wainwright inside. In her bright, multicolored striped dress and with her gray hair standing out in frizzy curls, Mrs. Wainwright reminded Miranda of a friendly, exotic bird.

"I'll be with you in a moment," she said. "I have a student with me now—she'll be done in five minutes."

She led them down a narrow hallway and showed them into the living room. "Please sit down. Make yourselves comfortable. My goodness, but it's hot!" She whirled out of the room. A moment later, tentative notes from a flute sounded from the back of the house.

"She seems okay," said Miranda.

Helen settled herself into an overstuffed, flowered armchair. "Yes, she's very friendly."

Miranda roamed around the small, tidy room. "Mither, look at this." She held up a large notebook that had lain on an end table. *The History of Garnet Township, 1691 to the Present*, by E. H. Wainwright. Is that *her*, do you think?" She thumbed through the pages. "Oh, look, they're all handwritten!"

"Oh my, yes indeed," said Mrs. Wainwright, returning and hurrying over to remove the book from Miranda's hands. She laughed. "You've found me out already! I'm the town's amateur historian — historian of the Ladies' Guild. We work to preserve the old flavor of the town — lots of potluck suppers, summer picnics, and the like. No McDonald's here!" She peered at Helen. "Mrs. Browne? Perhaps you would be interested in joining our society?"

Helen smiled. "Let me get settled into my office first," she said. "But I'd love to help with a potluck supper sometime."

"Oh, yes, you're a doctor, aren't you? So it isn't Mrs. Browne, but Dr. Browne. Didn't someone tell me just the other day — you're a pediatrician, isn't that it?"

"A gynecologist-obstetrician, actually. And please call me Helen."

"Well, Helen, I must say I'm pleased to see what women do these days. Delivering babies — my land!" Mrs. Wainwright beamed at her. "Though when you think about it, delivering babies is what women have always done, isn't it? I myself have been a working woman for fifty years, even when I was married, although my husband always complained. I think he was secretly proud of me, when it comes down to it, though. A good man, Nathan. He passed on five years ago. And now my music lessons help me out a lot." She frowned at Miranda. "You play the piano?"

Miranda held up her flute case.

"Ah, yes. That's lovely. Come along and play me a tune . . . Come into the music room. Yes, Dr. Browne — Helen — she'll be back in a bit . . ."

Miranda trailed after her down the hall, smiling at this chatter. She had no doubt she would play well for Mrs. Wainwright, despite her lack of practice since they'd moved to Garnet.

And she did play well, standing in front of the bay window, staring out across the garden. She played a Vivaldi piece, light and airy, all clear, strong notes and lilting runs, perfect summer music for a beautiful summer day.

"Lovely," nodded Mrs. Wainwright when the last long note died away. "You must have had a good teacher in New York. How long have you studied?"

Miranda straightened at this praise. "Four years."

"Ah," said Mrs. Wainwright. "A late starter." She laughed at Miranda's expression. "Yes, dear. I like to start my students as early as four or five. It trains breath control. In Japan, you know, children learn to play the violin when they're only two years old! I don't see why it shouldn't be the same for flute players. But you play very well, and I'll be happy to teach you what I know."

"Thank you," said Miranda.

"No need to thank me. Just make sure you do your practicing. I don't like laziness. Just keep that in mind, and remember: the key words are *breath control*."

Miranda and Helen drove away, waving out the window to Mrs. Wainwright, who stood on the porch. "See you Wednesday!" she called after them in her airy, flute-like voice.

"It'll work out perfectly," said Helen. "I can pick you up on Wednesdays right after work — once I start working, that is. Until then, you can ride your bike."

"Okay," agreed Miranda, already making plans to go early that week. It had occurred to her that anyone who had lived in Garnet so long and was historian for the Ladies' Guild as well might know something about the dollhouse families. The Hootons and their museum could be useful, too.

At the library Miranda filled out a form for a borrower's card. Then she wandered around, looking at the displays of books. "Books for Browsers." "Summertime Romances." "Gardening." On a shelf marked "Local Literature" she found a book titled *Small-Town Massachusetts in Pictures*. She decided it might be fun to read, even if it didn't yield any information about her house. But then her eye caught another title: *Garnet Township in the Nineteenth Century.* She removed it from the shelf and was surprised to see the author's name: E. H. Wainwright. So Mrs. Wainwright was not such an amateur as she made out! Miranda leafed through the book, then carried it to the check-out desk.

Philip announced at dinner that he wanted to return to New York for the weekend to attend his last session at the weight-loss clinic. "They're having a party for me," he laughed. "But no munchies — we'll all be there sipping mineral water!"

"I wouldn't want to miss it for the world," Helen told him. "I'm so proud of you, Phil."

"We'll leave in the morning," he said.

Miranda had no choice but to go with them. She didn't miss the look of relief her parents exchanged across the table when she said she'd like to see Nicole again. They'd clearly expected her to dig her heels in about leaving the house. *Maybe I have been up with that dollhouse too much*, she thought.

While she was flinging some clothes into a tote bag for the trip to New York, the telephone rang.

Helen answered in the kitchen, but Miranda heard her exclamations all the way upstairs. She ran down to listen. "Willy! Hello! How wonderful to hear from you! Where *are* you?"

Willy was Helen's younger brother. "Where?" she asked. "All of you? Well, of course! That's no problem at all. You wouldn't believe how much room we have now... You know you're welcome wherever we are! When will you come?"

In a short while she hung up and looked across the table at Philip. "That was Willy. He and Belle and the kids are on their way—they'll be here in a few *hours,* can you believe it? It's just like him to arrive out of the blue. They're just north of here now."

"But that's great!" cried Miranda, coming into the kitchen. "How long will they stay?" These Maine relatives had always been favorites of hers, but the families rarely seemed to find time to get together.

"Just the weekend, they said. They're on their way out west to Yellowstone. Oh, Phil—wait—what about your party? I'll miss it!"

"Oh well, it isn't much, I guess. Just a bunch of former fatties applauding someone else who has made it into the ranks."

"Oh, Phil!" Helen reached over to hug him. "It's a big deal! And I do want to come. Look, I'll call Willy back. I don't want to miss your party—"

"Never mind," he said. "Really."

"But I'm so proud of you! I should be at the party."

"It is a big loss," he agreed, but now his voice was teasing. "Think of all that mineral water you'll miss."

"Well, *I'll* come to your party, Dad!"

"No, you both stay here, and stop worrying about it. Maybe I'll invite some of the folks out here for a weekend soon. They'd enjoy getting away from the city, and we can celebrate all over again."

"Maybe Nicole could come, too," Miranda suggested.

"That's a good idea," said Helen. "In fact, how about if Dad brings Nicole back to Garnet with him on Sunday? She could stay the whole next week, if her parents don't mind."

"Oh, Mither, that will be fun!"

"Willy will be here soon—and I still haven't unpacked everything," fretted Helen. "I don't even know where the extra pillows are!"

Miranda ticked the people off on her fingers. "Aunt Belle, Uncle Willy, Anni, and Simon. That's only four pillows, Mither," she said in a comforting voice. "Nothing to get all nervous about."

"It's just that they always arrive virtually unannounced, and I usually have a million other things on my mind."

"I like that," said Miranda. "It's nice and spontaneous. After all, they're *family*—nothing out of the ordinary!"

# 5

Uncle Willy, Aunt Belle, Anni, and Simon arrived full of good humor and famished for the after-supper snack Helen and Miranda laid out — cold chicken, pickles, French bread, and wild strawberries from the garden. The sleeping arrangements turned out not to be a problem; Uncle Willy had arrived driving a camper.

Anni, who was six, and Simon, who was seven, screeched their greetings as they raced from the camper into Miranda's arms.

"You sure are lucky!" Anni told Miranda after everyone had been given a tour of the new house, and they were sitting outside on the porch.

"And what a lovely garden," added Aunt Belle. "Our garden in Maine is impossibly rocky, but you could grow almost anything in this soil."

"The garden is a bit wild," said Philip, "but I have plans to tame it."

"Such a strong smell of magnolia," commented

Aunt Belle. She rubbed her eyes and pressed her fingers to her temples.

Without warning the terror began.

Everyone looked just as they had a moment before, and everything was the same as it had been all evening, yet the air around Miranda suddenly grew heavy and the fear became palpable. Her dry mouth yearned for a sip of water, anything. Her thin body broke out in a sweat, tensing against an unknown evil. Her hands gripped her knees. Around her, faintly, she heard the buzz of light conversation, the clink of ice in glasses. *Help me, oh God, helpmehelpmehelpme . . .*

Who had said that? She couldn't breathe. Why didn't anyone notice? She tried to speak and failed. Her parched lips would crack if she opened her mouth. This was a hundred times worse than the terror that sometimes assailed her at the dollhouse. There she could look away, turn it off, control it. Here it encircled her. She was frozen in place with no one to run to. She tried again to scream, but though her mother sat only a few feet away, she didn't seem to hear.

"Mither!" It burst out at last, not the scream Miranda heard in her own head, but a small gasp, almost a sigh.

Helen and Aunt Belle looked up and smiled. "Hmm? Did you say something, Mandy?" Helen asked.

But at the sound of her mother's voice the terror was gone. Miranda relaxed and unclenched her hands. "I guess not," she murmured.

Miranda phoned Nicole before she went to bed that night. She had to hold the receiver at arm's length to protect her ear from her friend's shrieks of excitement at the invitation. So Philip left alone for New York the following morning, planning to return Sunday evening with Nicole.

Miranda spent the morning hanging out in the garden with Anni and Simon. When Simon had the idea to shift the masses of ivy and brambles to make a hiding place among some boxwood bushes, the girls pitched in. Miranda made thick peanut butter and peach jam sandwiches, and they ate them in the hollowed-out space, enjoying the coolness of the shaded ground. Helen, Aunt Belle, and Uncle Willy drove into town after lunch to window-shop.

Anni and Simon, tiring of outdoor play, talked Miranda into a game of hide-and-seek. They agreed that anywhere in the house would be within limits. The dining room table was goal. Miranda searched for a place to hide. As she passed the door that led to the attic, she opened it and stepped quickly inside. She sat down on the bottom step, leaving the door open a crack, and waiting silently. Soon she grew bored. Playing with her younger cousins had tired her out, and she wanted to be alone.

The dollhouse! She felt it beckoning, as if her absence had been noticed, her observation missed. She stood and started up the stairs, then halted. If she went up, her cousins would find her there. She didn't want to share her strange secret with them. She steeled herself against the lure of the dollhouse and sat back down on the steps, feeling restless in the hot, still air.

She thought longingly of the cool space they'd cleared under the boxwood bushes. Why didn't anybody come? Where was Simon? He was "it," wasn't he? Surely she had not chosen such a hard place to find. How thirsty she was! The stairway walls seemed to close in on her, and still no one came ... Just as she stood up to declare the game over in disgust and run downstairs for some frosty lemonade, the terror hit her. It hit her with real force, throwing her back down on the steps and leaving her gasping for breath. She couldn't move. Cries reverberated in her head, in the air, seeming to come from the attic overhead. *Help me!*

Had she cried out herself? But she could not open her mouth, could not even stand up again. *Paralyzed — oh, God! I'm going to die*, she thought quite clearly. She began to tremble violently.

And then, as suddenly as it had begun, the terror was gone — as if it had never been there at all — and Miranda ran downstairs. Helen, Uncle Willy, and Aunt Belle were just returning from their trip into town. She threw herself into her mother's arms, sobbing with remembered fear and the relief that she *could* cry, that she was not dead. But even in finally telling her mother what had happened, she held back about the dollhouse, about her sense that it was calling to her. The dollhouse was *hers;* in some way she felt she had made a promise not to betray its secrets.

Helen listened quietly as Miranda spilled out the horror of the steps, with her eyes still wide and her lips trembling. Then the two of them went up together and sat on the attic steps. But the terror did not return. Miranda felt bewildered and a bit foolish, but Helen wasn't laughing.

"Sometimes things happen," she began slowly. "Girls your age . . . Well, when your body starts changing, you can get funny emotions. When I was your age I used to feel overwhelmingly sad, all of a sudden, and start bawling for absolutely no reason — and then just as suddenly the sadness would be gone. Maybe your terror is something like that." She patted Miranda's knee.

"Hormones, huh?" said Miranda, her voice still shaky.

"You've had a lot of changes in your life lately, Mandy. And I think you've been alone too much since we moved here. I know it's great to be away from New York crowds, but maybe you need to get out more. Do things with Dan Hooton, why don't you? Go bike riding. He seems nice enough."

"Okay," promised Miranda. The remnant of terror receded.

Aunt Belle had a headache and spent the rest of the afternoon lying in Helen and Philip's room with the door closed and a cool cloth on her forehead.

Evening found them all gathered once more on the porch, catching each other up on all the family news. They sat in the same places they had the night before, as if each seat had been assigned by some invisible teacher: Aunt Belle in the wicker rocker by the front door, Uncle Willy across from her. Helen sat in one corner of the couch with the green-and-white–checked cushions. The other corner, where Philip had sat, was empty. Miranda sat with her cousins in a row on the creaky green-cushioned swing at the end of the porch. Only Miranda's legs were long enough for her feet to touch the porch floor, which was covered with a long straw runner, so she was in charge of kicking the swing back and forth with her toe. The creak of the swing mingled with the click-clack-click of Aunt Belle's knitting needles.

Aunt Belle knitted furiously. Miranda had never known her to be without a piece of knitting nearby— sweaters for everyone in bright, warm winter colors that seemed too hot to touch on a summer's night, made from thick wool that she carried around in the deep pockets of her sundress.

Back and forth creaked the swing as Miranda's toe moved it. Click-clack-click whispered Aunt Belle's needles in the growing darkness of the porch. Background noises intruded now and then: an occasional car whisking past beyond the screen of bushes, chirps of crickets in the trees, and shouts of Dan and Buddy playing Frisbee tag across the road. Uncle Willy's cigarette glowed in the dusk. Miranda and Helen met each other's eyes and grinned: if Philip were home, Uncle Willy would be in for a lecture on the evils of nicotine.

"When I was little," said Uncle Willy, "we kids used to rock in a swing just like that, and once we rocked so hard and fast, it tipped right over backwards into the bushes. Remember, Helen?"

Miranda continued rocking. Anni and Simon

squirmed on the seat next to her. "Well, were you hurt?" asked Anni.

"Nope," he said. "But your Aunt Helen broke her nose."

Miranda's eyes widened. "You never told me about that, Mither!"

Helen was smiling at her brother. "I'd forgotten all about it."

Aunt Belle glanced at them, unusually silent. She began working a new color into the sweater she was knitting for Anni.

"Well, it was a long time ago," Uncle Willy said.

"How old were you?" asked Anni.

"About as old as you are now, little dumpling." Uncle Willy's friendly laugh boomed out in the darkness. Anni scowled at the pet name, a relic from her plump babyhood.

When Miranda was younger she had often wished rather guiltily that Aunt Belle and Uncle Willy were her parents, Simon and Anni her brother and sister, and their house on the rocky Maine coast her house, too. She wished this when life in their tiny New York apartment seemed stifling, when her parents were busy with their work, when the gray city streets depressed her.

Uncle Willy was full of jokes and stories, and he never tired of playing with his children. Aunt Belle was gentle and cheerful, and she spoke with a drawling southern accent even though she'd lived in Maine for years. Miranda had often tried to mimic Aunt Belle's soft voice, but she could never manage to keep from laughing. Aunt Belle tried to coach her. "The trick," she said, "is to make all one-syllable words have two syllables, and all two-syllable words have three, and so on." They had both dissolved in laughter at Miranda's attempts.

"Mom," said Anni suddenly, breaking the stillness on the porch and jolting Miranda out of her musing. "Can me and Simon and Mandy go play with those kids?" She jumped off the swing.

"*Can* who play with those children?"

"Me and Simon and Mandy."

"*Think*, young lady," snapped Aunt Belle.

Miranda's eyes widened. She had *never* heard Aunt Belle snap before.

Uncle Willy raised his eyebrows at Aunt Belle and pulled Anni to him. "Your grammar, dumpling."

"All right, *may* I play with them?" Anni squirmed away from him, losing patience.

"And who else?" Aunt Belle's voice was still cold, still not her own.

"May Mandy and Simon and I."

"That's better." She settled back to her knitting. Click-clack-click. She smiled at her husband.

"Well, dearest Mother?" persisted Anni, sarcastic now.

Aunt Belle stopped smiling. "I don't know about Miranda, but you may not. We don't know them."

Helen laughed apologetically. "We don't know the boys well—Mandy has been too busy—but we were over at their house the other evening ..." Her voice trailed off. "I've spoken with their mother several times. They live just across the street in that old house that's the Garnet Museum now. They're perfectly nice boys."

Simon pulled on Miranda's hand. "C'mon, then. Let's go!"

Aunt Belle's knitting needles stopped abruptly. "I said no, Simon. You stay away from those children, do you hear me?"

Uncle Willy glanced sharply at Aunt Belle. "What's with you? Of course they can go play!" He nodded to Simon. "Go ahead, kids."

Miranda stretched in the swing. "You two go on. I'll sit here."

Anni scowled. "Why is everybody being so weird?"

"I'm not! I just want to sit here. Maybe later."

"Later you three children shall all be put to bed," said Aunt Belle angrily.

Miranda bristled at the cold, formal tone. What was eating Aunt Belle? She felt her own temper rise. "I'm thirteen years old," she snapped. "No one puts me to bed!"

"Mandy—," chided Helen.

Simon and Anni leaped down the creaky steps into the yard. Behind the bushes and the magnolia tree their laughter and shrieks rang gaily. Miranda turned sideways on the swing and put her feet up. Something seemed wrong here. She felt out of place. She wished she had gone with her father. If she had, she would be safe and cool in the Rosenbaums' tiny, air-conditioned apartment.

Safe? Odd word. She was safe here, of course. Yet, there *was* something. She couldn't put her finger on

66

it. Everything seemed normal enough—except for Aunt Belle's bad temper—and yet the air was different. Charged, somehow. She tried to pinpoint it. Sort of like the fear she'd felt last night and on the attic steps today. A tension—like the first stages of the dollhouse terror: an intensified awareness of the slightest nuances in voices and atmosphere.

But how could she feel terror in such an ordinary setting? This was a cozy family reunion. She wasn't even alone. A porch. Her aunt, uncle, and mother talking softly in the dusk. Ice clinking in drinks. A June evening, tree frogs everywhere, and the sweet smell of magnolia blossoms.

The smell of magnolia blossoms.

Something nudged Miranda's memory. Terror and the smell of magnolias? Miranda rubbed her eyes. No connection there—and yet, and yet there was *something* . . .

"Mither?"

"Hmm?"

"Mither, come sit with me."

Helen smiled and stood up, smoothing her pleated summer skirt, and sat down again next to Miranda on the swing. She drew her long legs up under her skirt and circled Miranda's narrow shoulders with one arm. She smelled of fresh air. Miranda leaned her head on Helen's shoulder, eyes closed. They rocked gently.

A red Frisbee landed with a clatter on the porch floor, and Buddy's face appeared in the bushes by the porch railing. "Oops!" he laughed. "That was out of bounds."

Uncle Willy leaned over, retrieved the Frisbee, and sailed it out over the bushes. "Here you go, fella."

"Thanks!"

There was laughter in the bushes, and Simon's fair head appeared next to Buddy's. He waved the Frisbee. "Thanks, Dad. I guess I threw it too far. Don't know my own strength!"

With a low sound in her throat, Aunt Belle was on her feet. "Simon!" Miranda jerked her head off Helen's shoulder, startled by the venom in Aunt Belle's voice. "You come up here right now, young man! And where is Anni?"

"She's right here," said Simon in a small, uncertain voice.

Buddy looked from Simon to his mother, then lifted the Frisbee from Simon's hands. "Guess you gotta go," he said, shrugging. "See you later."

"Get back up on this porch this instant," hissed Aunt Belle. "Didn't I say you weren't to play with those street children? Didn't I warn you?"

"Belle!" began Uncle Willy, but Aunt Belle was off the porch already, pulling Anni by the arm and herding Simon up the steps in front of her.

"Now you two are in for it," she stormed. "I won't be disobeyed!" She sat down heavily in her chair, still holding Anni by the arm. Even in the semi-darkness, Miranda could see that Anni had turned white under her tan.

Aunt Belle pushed Simon toward Uncle Willy. "Well, William, I trust you to take your son in hand. Flagrant disobedience! I won't have it!"

Simon grabbed his father's hand. "Dad! What's wrong with her? We didn't do anything—!"

He broke off as Aunt Belle raised a hand and slapped him across the cheek.

Uncle Willy gathered the sobbing boy into his arms and glowered at Aunt Belle. "I think," he said in a tight voice, "it's time for us all to go get ready for bed." He stood up. "Come on, Anni."

Simon shuffled down the steps and over to the camper parked in the driveway. Helen cleared her throat, frowning. "*Really,* Belle! What in the world is wrong? There was no harm in it. Willy told the kids they could play—and the Hooton boys are nice—"

Aunt Belle still held Anni tightly. "Harm in it? I don't know about that. But the simple issue is that I won't have my children playing with street children. I will not have it said that my children are common."

"Come on, Belle, let's go," said Uncle Willy. Helen set her lips.

"Go on over with Simon, Anni," said Uncle Willy, when Aunt Belle did not move.

"No!" Aunt Belle's voice was razor sharp.

The stillness on the porch was complete. Miranda sensed, rather than saw, the icy glitter of Aunt Belle's eyes. Aunt Belle stood suddenly and crossed to where Miranda and Helen sat in the swing. Miranda shrank back. Aunt Belle lifted the unoccupied corner cushion of the swing and removed one of the thin wooden slats that supported the cushion. She turned to Anni, who backed away.

"Belle!" Helen jumped up.

"You stay out of this, Helen," warned Aunt Belle. "You handle your daughter the way you like, and leave me to mine."

Miranda squeezed her eyes shut.

"All right, then, young miss." And with that, Aunt Belle turned the child over her knee and lifted the slat. Anni let out a strangled cry. In an instant, Uncle Willy seized her from Aunt Belle's grip and guided her away, down off the porch into the night. Miranda could hear Anni's sobs from the camper. Another sound broke in, too: the sharp, hard hits of wood on flesh as Aunt Belle, who sat staring over the bushes, smacked the slat into her hand again and again and again — and then the chorus of crickets and tree frogs resumed, and the smell of magnolia was everywhere. The smell of magnolia! A closed feeling bore down on Miranda, stifling her — the feeling of having been here before, exactly so, but differently so — and the terror rising to her throat paralyzed her limbs. A deep moan escaped from her throat.

Helen grabbed Aunt Belle's wrist as the slat came down on her palm again.

"That's *enough,* Belle!" she shouted and threw the slat clattering onto the floor.

Aunt Belle sucked in her breath and stared at her reddened palm. There was silence on the porch for the space of a heartbeat. "Oh, my God," Aunt Belle whispered.

The scent of magnolia blossoms was very strong. And Miranda was thirsty.

# 6

Early the next morning the visitors prepared to leave. Uncle Willy sat in the driver's seat looking drawn; Anni and Simon sat quietly in the back. Uncharacteristically, Anni sucked her thumb. Aunt Belle was still in the house with Helen. Uncle Willy honked his horn for her to hurry.

Miranda walked over to the window on Uncle Willy's side. "Have a good trip," she said, not knowing what else to say. No one seemed to know what to say this morning.

"Thanks, honey." His voice was distant.

"The geysers should be fantastic." It was terrible the way no one met anyone else's eyes.

Uncle Willy tapped the horn again shortly and looked toward the house. Helen and Aunt Belle were coming down the porch steps, Helen's arm around Aunt Belle's waist. Miranda moved away from the camper, closer to her mother and Aunt Belle.

"I don't think you should let yourself get too upset

about it," Helen was murmuring. "It happened, but no one was hurt, and it isn't so bad you all won't get over it."

"How can I face them, Helen? I'm a monster." Aunt Belle's voice sounded hollow. "Oh, Helen, please believe me. I have never — I never even spanked one of them! You can ask Anni and Simon! What kind of mother would try to do what I wanted to do — and I wanted to, Helen. That's the part I don't understand — I wanted to hurt her! Only a monster would act that way."

"Calm down, Belle. You're no more a monster than I am!"

Aunt Belle did not seem to hear. She spoke listlessly. "It was as if *I* weren't even really saying those things — it was as if I were listening to a stranger . . ." Her voice trailed off as they reached Miranda. Aunt Belle looked down at the ground, and Miranda suddenly felt sorry for her. Aunt Belle climbed into the camper next to Uncle Willy.

The bustle of good-byes began, but they were hushed, not the boisterous good wishes that usually accompanied departing members of the family.

"Thank you so much, Helen."

"Give our love to Phil — I'm sorry we can't wait till he comes home." The big vehicle lurched backward ever so slightly as Uncle Willy shifted into gear.

"Helen!" Aunt Belle unceremoniously leaned across him in an attempt to reach the window. "Helen, please listen to me. What I told you last night — it's true! It's the *house*."

"Belle! What are you talking about?" Uncle Willy stomped on the brake pedal and pushed her back against the seat. "What's *wrong* with you?" he fairly hissed. "First that outrageous scene last night, and now we're treated to more of your theatrics!"

"Willy," she began, touching his arm helplessly, leaning across him again to the window where Helen and Miranda stood. "Helen, I'm sorry. I am *so* sorry. I don't know what happened to me, I never — "

Anni and Simon glanced at each other, then bent down to search for a game to play on the trip.

"Enough, Belle!" Uncle Willy backed the camper slowly. "Bye, Mandy; bye, Helen. Belle! Sit down, for God's sake!"

The camper swung out onto the road. Helen and Miranda raised their arms to wave, and Belle's last broken cry reached their ears: "It's the house — !"

As the camper disappeared around the bend, Helen and Miranda dropped their arms. Helen's shoulders sagged.

"Mither? What did she mean about the house?"

"I don't know, Mandy. She stayed in our room with me all night. She said she was afraid."

"Afraid of what? Of Uncle Willy?"

"N-no." Helen hesitated. "I think she was afraid of — of herself."

"Herself?" Miranda pondered this for a moment. "Afraid that she might try to hurt someone else, you mean?"

They spoke quietly, hesitantly, as if afraid voicing

such thoughts would bring back the trauma of the previous night. Helen ran her hands through her curly hair.

"She didn't sleep all night. Every time I woke up and looked at her, she was just staring at the ceiling. I asked her what was wrong—and she said we should get out of here."

"Get out?"

"Move out of this house. She said she felt it wasn't safe."

"But, *why*, Mither?"

Helen turned an anguished face to Miranda. "Oh, Mandy, you saw what happened to Belle last night. You saw what she tried to do to Anni! Belle is the most gentle person in the world—you know that as well as I do. She would never lift a finger to one of her own children. I don't understand. It wasn't like Belle. It doesn't make sense."

"But why did she say our house isn't safe?" Miranda continued to probe.

Helen touched Miranda's cheek. "Belle thinks the *house* wanted her to beat Anni. And she thinks we should move so that the house won't make us hurt each other."

Miranda shivered in the hot morning sun. "I don't get it. That sounds crazy."

Helen bit her lip and stared at the house. The sun glinted gold off the attic windows. "I don't get it, either," she said and turned to go inside.

———

That night Philip arrived home with Nicole. After exuberant rejoicing in the downstairs hall, the two girls carried Nicole's suitcase up to Miranda's bedroom.

"I can't believe this! I demand a tour of your mansion right this second," said Nicole. "Our whole apartment would fit in your bedroom!"

They set off through the rooms. Nicole's excited exclamations—"Oh, it's beautiful! What a huge fireplace! How cool. A garden with real trees...and all those flowers!"—made Miranda feel proud, as if she herself were personally responsible for the spaciousness of the rooms and the wild abundance of the garden. As they returned to Miranda's room, they passed the attic door. Nicole stopped, her hand on the knob. "What's in here?"

"Oh, that's just to the storage area." She felt the same reluctance now that she'd felt with Anni and Simon. No one must go into the attic. It was hers alone.

Nicole flung open the door. "Oh! Storage! This goes to the attic." She started up the steps. "Let's see."

"Well, we do store stuff up here ...," Miranda muttered hesitantly, following along behind her. Then, suddenly, the lure of the attic reached out to Miranda, practically pulling her up the stairs. But Nicole stopped abruptly at the top.

"Never mind! Let's forget it."

"What?"

"Let's go down."

"Why? What's the matter?"

"Nothing." Nicole shrugged her shoulders and mustered a careless tone. "It's just—dark."

Miranda flicked on the light. "Begone, spooks!"

Nicole stepped cautiously into the attic and peered around the big room. "Not much to see. Let's go back downstairs."

But Miranda moved across the room to the doll-house as if pulled by a string. Nicole followed. "Oh!" she cried. "It's an exact copy of *this* house, isn't it?"

Miranda crouched behind the house and looked into the dollhouse attic without answering. Nicole was standing directly on the other side, marveling at the tiny details of brick and ornate porch railings, panes of glass, the brass door knocker. But through the attic windows Miranda could not see her. Instead she was looking into the whitewashed attic playroom of the little girl. Miranda felt the rightness of being back with the house, and she sank slowly onto her knees, keeping her eyes riveted on the tiny attic. Snow fell outside the windows in thick flakes. The room was empty, but Miranda heard footsteps clattering up the stairs and the shrill sound of a child's wailing.

"Nicole," whispered Miranda. "Come look at this!"

The attic door was thrown open, and the regal-looking woman Miranda remembered from the 1904 kitchen stormed into the room trailing an overpowering scent of magnolia perfume and dragging little Dorothy by the arm. The girl wore only a thin white petticoat and was shivering from cold as well as fear.

"Oh!" gasped Miranda as the sickening terror washed over her, pounding at her temples. She clenched her teeth and did not turn away.

"Mandy!" Nicole's voice, sharp and worried,

reached her ears. "Hey! What's wrong with you?"

"Ssshhh!" hissed Miranda, fighting down nausea and not taking her eyes from the scene. "Wait a minute and watch!"

"Watch *what?* What are you doing?"

"I'll just be a minute."

Dorothy fell to the floor as her mother shoved her into the room. "Mama!" she shrieked.

"I've had it with you." Lucinda's cold voice made Miranda shiver. "I don't want any more nonsense. Now stay up here until you can be a pleasant, well-mannered child."

"I'm going down, Mandy." Nicole's voice came from far away. She sounded angry. "I'm going to have your dad take me back to New York tonight—right away!"

"Oh, wait, Nicole! Look through the attic windows—"

"What's *wrong* with you?"

"Sssshhh! Shut up!"

Lucinda stepped back from the crying child and smoothed her hands over the skirt of her dressing gown. "Dorothy," she said to the crumpled child at her feet. "You will stay here until you can learn deport-ment. I will not have a clumsy, disobedient child in this house!" She stalked across to the door, the heavy robe swishing behind her. A moment later she was out of the room, pulling the door shut. An iron key grated in the lock. In a flash Dorothy was on her feet, flying to the door.

"Mama, Mama!" she screamed, kicking the heavy door with her small, bare feet. "Let me out!"

At that moment Miranda was wrenched sharply

away from the dollhouse. Nicole glared at her, one hand tight on Miranda's T-shirted shoulder.

"Miranda Browne, you are the *worst* hostess in the world!" she shouted. "I come all the way from New York to visit you and instead of talking to me, you sit up in a spooky old attic and stare into a stupid dollhouse!"

"Nicole, I'm sorry ..." Miranda felt a bright flush start up her cheeks. "I was just—"

"Just *nothing!* You were totally ignoring me!"

"No, I was watching—" She stopped and lowered her head. "I'm really sorry, Nicole."

"I thought we were still best friends, Mandy!" Nicole stormed out of the attic and clattered down the stairs.

Miranda hesitated, hating herself for having been rude, yet wanting to stay at the dollhouse to learn what happened to poor little Dorothy. She stooped for one last look but encountered only the black-curtained attic windows of the other family. Sighing, she brushed off her shorts and hurried down the steps after Nicole.

She found her friend in the living room. Helen and Philip looked up when Miranda entered the room, and Philip put aside the magazine he had been reading. "Mandy," he began, "Nicole is very upset—"

"Please don't go," Miranda begged. "I was just—daydreaming! I'm sorry. I *said* I was sorry."

"You looked like you were watching television or something," Nicole said in a small voice.

"Please stay, dear," said Helen. "Mandy has apologized, and I'm sure she didn't mean to be rude. *I* know — why don't you come with me to the kitchen, and we'll make everyone a snack. Then you and Mandy can start catching up on each other's news."

Nicole followed her out of the room, looking back once at Miranda.

Philip shut the living-room door. "What's up, Mandy?"

Miranda shrugged.

"You've been spending an awful lot of time up in that attic," he pressed. "Why?"

"I just like it."

"Well, look. We've invited Nicole for the whole week — and I'm going to ask you to stay out of the attic until she's gone. How about it? You two must be able to find plenty to do around here without having to sit up in the attic."

She couldn't let him see how great a sacrifice it would be to stay away from the dollhouse that long. She shrugged again. "Sure, Dad. Don't worry." But she knew she'd have to go to the attic. It was like an addiction, this fascination of hers. Forbidden or not, she must watch.

In the kitchen, Miranda pulled out a chair at the table and plucked a grape from Helen's edible centerpiece. Nicole kept her back to Miranda and stood at the stove watching Helen fry cheese sandwiches in the heavy skillet. Philip sat across the table from Miranda; just above his head was the exact place where the 1904 calendar hung. *Had hung*, Miranda corrected herself mentally. Past tense. An uncomfortable silence filled the kitchen; no one spoke until the smell of burning bread wafted through the room and Helen exclaimed, "Damn! I've burned yours, Mandy!"

The stove stood in the same corner of the kitchen where Lucinda's cast-iron "monster" had stood. The smell of burning bread was the same smell that permeated this same kitchen almost eighty-five years ago. The sense of déjà vu left Miranda feeling giddy. "What do you mean, you burned 'mine.' Do I get a special one?"

"Yours doesn't have any tomatoes, of course."

"It doesn't? Why not?"

"You don't like tomatoes. You know that, Mandy."

"What are you talking about, Mither?" Miranda stared at Helen. "I love tomatoes!"

Helen glanced over her shoulder. "Nonsense. You've always hated tomatoes."

Miranda's eyes widened. Tomatoes were her very favorite vegetable. Helen had, in fact, bought extra tomato plants for the garden just to satisfy Miranda. If Helen had said Miranda didn't like chocolate cake or flute music, Miranda could not have been more surprised. "Mither," she said softly. "I've always *loved* tomatoes. Spaghetti with your homemade Bolognese sauce is my favorite dinner." She turned to Philip. "Right, Dad?"

He nodded.

There was another long silence in the kitchen. Miranda looked at her mother's stony face and her father's clouded one. She wasn't sure what made her say what she said next: "Dad, do you think old houses keep the personalities of people who once lived in them?"

"Like ghosts, you mean?" asked Nicole.

"No, not exactly. I mean, do you think an old house can have a special atmosphere?"

Philip smiled slightly. "I suppose so, Mandy, but I don't know how the house would get the atmosphere in the first place. I mean, through the years so many people live in a single house before it falls to pieces — you couldn't have impressions left of all of them ... or could you? I don't know."

"Well, have you noticed that our house has an atmosphere?" Out of the corner of her eye, she noticed Helen had grown quite pale.

"What kind of atmosphere?" asked Philip, becoming interested.

"Well, a weird atmosphere. Like Aunt Belle said." Then she remembered her father had not heard Aunt Belle that morning. "She said it was the house that made her — "

At that moment Helen threw down the spatula and burst into tears. She ran from the kitchen. They heard her footsteps racing up the stairs. Philip shoved back his chair so forcefully that it knocked into the wall and tottered as if about to fall.

"You girls wait here," he commanded, hurrying from the room.

Nicole and Miranda stared at each other. "Want a sandwich?" offered Miranda finally, not knowing what else to say.

"Sure." Nicole reached for one.

Then the silence between them stretched into what seemed like minutes, until Nicole broke it with an uncomfortable laugh. "You seem really different, Mandy."

"Different from what?"

"From the way you were in New York."

"New York seems a long time ago."

"Come on! Less than a month."

Miranda reached for another sandwich. "How do you mean, then, 'different'?"

"Well, haven't you met any kids around here? Do you just sit around all the time?"

"Of course I've met kids. There are two boys just across the street—"

"Boys! How old?"

"Oh, one of them is little, around eight. The other is a year older than we are."

"Is he cute?"

Miranda tried to remember what Dan Hooton looked like. "I guess so. Uh—sure, he's okay. I don't really know him."

"Why not? Does he have a girlfriend already?"

Miranda shook her head. "I don't know. I mean—I haven't seen him much."

"See? That's what I mean. You are totally changed. I can't believe there is a boy across the street, and you don't have his life story yet! Back in the city—"

"It's different here."

"Like I said. And it's not just you. Your parents, too. What's all this about the house and atmosphere and weird stuff?"

Before Miranda could think of a response, Philip pushed through the swinging door, his arm around Helen's shoulders. Helen smiled sheepishly at the girls.

"I'm sorry," she said rather tremulously, sitting down at the table and reaching for a sandwich. "I don't know what got into me. Let's just try to forget it, please."

# 7

The girls spent the next week exploring the town and surrounding countryside, taking picnics to the fields and wading in streams. The morning after Nicole arrived, Philip had dragged Helen's old bike out of the stable and lowered the seat to fit Nicole. Miranda held her breath when her father walked toward the corner where the cushionless couch was, but he noticed nothing and rolled Miranda's bike out onto the grass. He had to raise the seat; she had grown several inches since she last rode it. Miranda oiled the chains on both bikes. "You're so lucky," Nicole said as they set off on their first ride. "There's no place to ride in the city."

Miranda popped up to the attic for a few minutes each day while Nicole was in the shower, but otherwise she fought against the lure of the dollhouse and tried to throw herself into the visit with Nicole.

It seemed Helen and Philip were arguing a lot that week. Miranda was embarrassed in front of her friend—her parents sounded like such *kids*. They'd hardly ever quarreled in New York, but here they bickered about what color to paint the dining room, whether the basement should be paneled to make a recreation room, who had eaten the last banana, and what time a certain film came on television. It seemed to Miranda that her mother often started the fights; Helen had been out-of-sorts and irritable ever since Uncle Willy's visit.

At the end of the week they argued about who should be the one to drive Nicole back to New York. They finally compromised by making it a day's visit for everyone.

Miranda entered the old apartment building without a single ounce of homesickness. Their life in New York seemed very remote. But Helen and Philip relaxed at the Rosenbaums' as they hadn't all week at home. They didn't quarrel even once—and seemed sorry when evening came and it was time to leave.

Helen drove skillfully through the city traffic and onto the highway back to Garnet. The farther they got from the city, the more intense the sniping became in the front seat. Finally Miranda set aside the book she'd been reading and leaned forward between the two front seats. "Hey, you guys. Let's play the alphabet game."

Philip smiled over his shoulder at her. "Good idea. Mandy saves the day!"

The game was quite simple; everyone tried to spot words beginning with each letter of the alphabet on billboards, signposts, or bumper stickers. But long-time devotees like the Brownes knew how difficult it was to get past _Q_. If, with luck, a sign urged "Quench

Your Thirst with Gatorade," the game would probably stop again on *X*, this time without hope.

Miranda spotted a billboard depicting a smiling young mother and father holding a fat baby. The baby brandished a blue box of Q-Tips.

"Q-Tips for the Whole Family!" cried Miranda. "That's *Q*!"

"Ow, Mandy!" Helen winced. "Don't yell in my ear."

"Sorry." She nudged her father, who was keeping score. "Q-Tips, Dad. Point for me."

"Humph," muttered Philip. "I don't know about that. We agreed not to use 'Grade A Milk' for *A* and 'No U Turn' for *U* last time because they're only single letters and not the beginning letters of words."

"No, it's the *name* of a thing," Miranda argued. "Q-Tips is a brand name."

"Well . . ."

"Ranger Station," said Helen without taking her eyes off the road. "*R* and *S*. Two points for me."

Philip grumbled. "Oh, all right. *Q* for Mandy. *R* and *S* for Helen. I'm just a sore loser."

As usual, they became stuck on *X* and discontinued the game.

"Why don't people sell xylophones along the side of the road?" asked Miranda.

Philip laughed. Helen swiped a hand across her eyes. "Do you have a headache?" Philip asked.

"Just a little one."

"Why don't you let me drive, then? We can stop right up the road there and change places."

"No, I'm fine." She rubbed her forehead. "We're almost home, anyway."

They were nearing Garnet. Helen piloted the car off the highway and onto the winding road leading them around Concord and through rich farmland. Another ten miles and they would be back in the new house. Home. Miranda stared out the window, trying to read the bumper stickers on cars as they whizzed past. "I Love New York," she announced. "Virginia Is for Lovers. Maryland Is for Crabs. Honk If You Love Jesus."

Helen massaged the back of her neck with one hand. "Quiet please, Miranda."

"Let me drive," urged Philip.

"I said I'm *fine*," she snapped.

"No need to get huffy, Helen. If you've got a headache, it's stupid to keep driving."

She whirled on him. "I told you I'm fine! Are you calling me stupid?"

"Keep your eyes on the road!" yelled Philip. "Yes! I call anyone stupid who insists on driving with a headache and who can't keep her eyes on the road! Stupid and dangerous!"

Miranda made herself small in the backseat and stared out the side window. It seemed the closer they got to Garnet, the more intense the atmosphere grew, closing in on all three of them. Her mother's mounting headache. This dumb quarrel.

A man driving a blue sports car blared his horn as he passed their swerving car on the narrow road. As he swung ahead of them, Miranda read the large yellow sticker on the back of his car: Honk If You Love Cheeses. She laughed aloud, and Helen glanced over her shoulder.

"What's wrong with you?" she inquired coldly.

Miranda stared at her. "Nothing!"

"What were you laughing at?"

Miranda sighed. "Oh, just something that seemed funny."

"I asked you *what,* young lady."

"God, Mither! A little while back I saw a bumper sticker that said, 'Honk If You Love Jesus.'" She tried to keep the rising temper out of her voice. "And just now I saw one saying 'Honk If You Love Cheeses.'" Having to explain made the whole thing less amusing. "I just thought it was funny," she said defensively. "I don't know why you have to make such a big deal of it."

"Probably an ad for a cheese store," said Philip. He lit a cigarette. "Clever."

Helen pursed her lips. "Phil! You quit!"

"Give me a break, Helen! I've been trying!"

"Tch." She reached over, plucked the cigarette from Philip's lips, and flung it out the open window. "Looks like you'd better try harder," she snapped.

*"That does it!"* roared Philip. "Stop this car right now. This *instant!"*

Helen jerked the car to the side of the road, stalling the engine.

"Get out." His voice was icy. "I'm driving the rest of the way. You're obviously not up to it."

"Just who do you think you are —," began Helen in a voice Miranda did not recognize. The voice was low, utterly cold.

"I said, *get out!*" Philip's voice rose sharply, and Helen clenched her fingers around the steering wheel, never taking her eyes from his stormy face. At that moment Miranda burst into wrenching sobs.

In one movement, Helen tore her hands from the wheel, turned in her seat, and slapped Miranda across the face. Philip caught Helen's hand as it flew back for yet another blow, and Miranda collapsed against the side window.

*"Helen!"*

"I won't have a whining child in this car!" she cried and jumped out the door, racing across the field next to where they were parked.

Philip leaped out in quick pursuit, weaving in and out among the rows of cornstalks growing tall in the summer sun. Miranda, tears streaming down her scarlet face, huddled in her corner and stared out after them. Through a shocked haze she read the white sign hanging from a roadside post just in front of their car:

WELCOME TO GARNET, MASSACHUSETTS.

# 8

A sort of family truce went into effect after that. Miranda spoke to her mother as little as possible, and she spent hours each day in the attic. Helen put up new violet-sprigged wallpaper in the dining room. Philip retreated to the backyard, hacking down the underbrush with a scythe.

Miranda helped him a few hours one morning, pulling weeds in the tangled garden out front until the overpowering scent of the sun-baked magnolia blossoms threatened to turn her stomach. Then she went inside and made a ham sandwich, which she ate standing at the kitchen counter. She stared at the wall where the 1904 calendar had hung in another time.

Helen entered through the swinging door from the dining room, carrying a bucket of wallpaper paste. She stopped when she saw Miranda.

"Don't forget your flute lesson."

"I haven't."

Helen washed her hands at the sink. "Change that

T-shirt before you go. I distinctly remember throwing it into the trash back in New York."

"It's my favorite." Miranda poured herself a glass of milk. She didn't want to talk to her mother. She had nothing to say to her after the scene in the car. There had been no apology.

"It may well be, but I don't want you looking like a slob at Mrs. Wainwright's."

Miranda drained her glass and didn't answer. She rinsed the glass and plate and turned to leave the kitchen.

"Mandy—" Helen's voice sounded choked.

"What?" The word came out like a stone.

Helen sagged. "Do you want a slice of watermelon? I've got some fresh in the refrigerator."

"No, thanks."

"I'll drive you to Mrs. Wainwright's. I should go in to the office, anyway. I'm going to start work in a couple of weeks, and there's still so much to do to get the place ready."

"No, thanks," Miranda repeated. "I'm taking my bike." She relished the chance to soar over the rolling roads into town.

"Oh . . ." Helen picked up her bucket and moved toward the door. "Well, have a good lesson. Be careful riding."

Miranda grabbed her flute case and ran out to the stable. She leaped onto her bicycle, taking care to nestle the case securely on top of her music books in the wicker basket before whirling out of the driveway, spraying gravel behind her. She did not change her T-shirt.

Miranda braked in front of the small white house. She had arrived a few minutes early and sat down on the porch steps to wait. After only a minute or two the screen door opened and a boy bounded out, banging the door behind him.

"Buddy!"

Buddy Hooton grinned. "Hi! We thought you'd moved away or something. I never see you around. Don't you ever come outside?"

"Never," she told him. These days, it was almost true. "Why are you here? Do you play the flute?"

He shook his head. "Mom thinks somebody in the family should be"—he hesitated, trying to remember the phrase—"musically inclined." He scowled. "She gave up on Dan years ago, so I'm the hope of the family. But really, I just come for the cookies."

"What do you play?" Miranda asked.

He groaned. "Piano." He said the word as if it were a dread disease his mother had exposed him to.

Miranda laughed. "I wouldn't put it past Mrs. Wainwright to make another Beethoven out of you yet."

"No way."

"I'm early—can I just go in?"

"Oh, sure. Aunt Ellie's got a big plate of cookies on the kitchen table for anyone who gets here early. I always do!"

"Mrs. Wainwright is your aunt?"

"Well, my dad's aunt, really," he amended. "Look, there's my mom—I've got to go! See you!"

Miranda waved as he climbed into the van at the curb, and he and Mrs. Hooton waved back. Flute music filtered out the screen door to the front steps where she waited. The notes sounded high and clear in the summer air, then faltered and stopped. After a pause, they began again.

She went inside and sat down at the kitchen table. She was just helping herself to a third cookie when Mrs. Wainwright fluttered in.

"Oh, me! What a surprise!" She fanned a hand over her heart. "I never heard you come in!" Today Mrs. Wainwright wore a bright green dress, and a multi-colored bandanna covered her wild gray curls. She looked more than ever like a bird, bright and spritely.

"I didn't mean to barge in," began Miranda uncertainly. "I saw Buddy and he said to wait here."

"Of course, of course. Well, now that you're settled with a snack, I think I'll just take a little break, too. Do you mind?"

"No, not at all," said Miranda, feeling foolish granting Mrs. Wainwright permission to sit down in her own kitchen.

"Iced tea, dear?" Mrs. Wainwright poured Miranda a large glass before she could say she didn't like iced tea.

"Uh, thank you."

Mrs. Wainwright stretched her spindly legs out under the table. "So tell me. How do you like Garnet?"

Miranda hesitated. "It's very—beautiful."

"Yes, yes, but how do you like living here? How do you like your new house?"

"It's nice to have so much more room than we did in New York."

Mrs. Wainwright settled back, regarding her with bright eyes. "Hmm," she said.

"Have you ever been to my house?" Miranda asked suddenly.

Mrs. Wainwright sipped her tea, her eyes on the ceiling. "Yes, but that must have been—let's see, during the war. World War II, you know."

Miranda nodded.

"My goodness, it's almost fifty years since I've been in that house! And, of course, I went there when I was a little girl to peek in the windows with my brothers when the house was empty."

"Who lived in our house during the war?"

"Oh, a nice young couple from Boston. Let's see, named Kramer. The woman was very pretty, and named after a flower. Let's see. Rose? No. Daisy? No . . . oh, I remember now—it was Iris! Lovely girl. And I don't recall the fellow's name, but he was a handsome man, very dark and tall."

"Andrew," murmured Miranda.

"That's it! Andrew Kramer. There were two little boys, too, but I don't know their names anymore, either. How time does fly. That family was here only a year, I think. I took over a casserole when they first arrived."

"Timmy and Jeff," murmured Miranda. She sipped her iced tea. It was better than she'd expected. She looked up again to find Mrs. Wainwright regarding her with raised eyebrows.

"How do you know the names of those children, dear?"

Miranda inspected her ice cubes. "Oh, I guess I just heard someone talking about them . . ."

"Oh? Now I wonder who. Not many folks in Garnet would remember the Kramers."

Miranda shrugged, then ventured another question. "Why did they leave so soon?"

Mrs. Wainwright allowed herself to be sidetracked. "Let's see. They came in the early forties . . . I know it was then because I was pregnant with Matthew when I went to visit them. Matthew was born just before they moved back to Boston. Matthew is my youngest," she told Miranda. "My three children are all married. I have two lovely grandchildren out in Colorado."

Miranda hoped Mrs. Wainwright would not bring out the photo albums. There were still so many questions she wanted to ask. "The Kramers," she prompted.

"Oh, yes. As I said, they didn't stay long. Weren't very happy here, as I recall. Family problems of one kind or another." She peered shrewdly at Miranda. "That old house of yours certainly hasn't had a history of happy families. I hope you and your family will change that."

Miranda seized on this eagerly. "Why wasn't the first family happy? Do you know anything about them?"

"Of course I know, dear! I'm historian for the Ladies' Guild, after all." She paused to refill her glass. "Before the Kramers lived in your house—and a good long while before, mind you, around the turn of the century—the Galworthy family lived there. In fact, that handsome Kramer man was related to the Galworthy family, too. The house is still known locally as the Galworthy House; a man named Ezra Galworthy built it for his bride way back in 1790 or thereabouts. I could check the records, if you like. But in any case, at the turn of *this* century, Sigmund Galworthy was a young lawyer here in town. He had grown up in that house and continued to live there after his parents died. He and his wife had a little girl, too. Ah, what a tragedy."

"What kind of tragedy?"

"A terrible accident. Mrs. Galworthy and the little girl were killed in a train wreck. The big wreck of '04 on the Boston–New York line. All the old-timers talked of nothing else. Not too much happens around these parts to talk about!"

Miranda's thoughts raced ahead. The family she saw in the 1904 house must be the Galworthys. The calendar on the wall said 1904. But that meant that the mother and daughter must have died in the wreck later that same year! "When did the crash happen? I mean, do you know which month?"

"It was in the winter. It must have been around— no, for certain—it was January. People said what a terrible beginning to the New Year that was. It must have been horrible. I myself wasn't born till 1910, but people still talked about the wreck years later as if it had happened only yesterday. A lot of families in Garnet had fathers and husbands and sons who took the train to the cities.

"My mother often took care of the little Galworthy girl when Mrs. Galworthy went shopping or visiting. My older brothers were close to her in age, and another neighbor of ours, Joey Johnston, was a special playmate of hers. The whole bunch of them used to play together. It seems their two favorite games were weddings — dressing up in my parents' old clothes — and Underground Railway.

"My brothers often talked about that little girl when I was growing up. Her death had a real effect on them — I guess the death of a friend will do that to you at any age. And poor little Joey Johnston. Apparently he went into some kind of shock when he heard she had been killed. He retreated into himself. It was a long time before he would make any new friends again. Maybe he thought friendship wasn't worth it, if friends were going to die..." She shook her gray head.

"Of course, as I said, all this happened before I was born. I never knew the Galworthys myself. But since I grew up just across the street, their empty house was always a reminder of the tragedy. It kept the talk going."

Miranda tried to absorb all the details of the story Mrs. Wainwright told her. That poor little girl! That poor woman! "What about the man — Mr. Galworthy? Did you know him?" she asked.

"That sad man. Grief-stricken, I think, all the rest

of his life. No, he never lived in the house after his wife and daughter died. He went crazy, in a way—he must have loved them both very much. They were all he had, and he couldn't bear to go back into the house for a long time after the wreck. He'd been at work when word of the accident reached him, but at first he kept insisting that his wife had not been on the train. After he went to identify her body, he was frantic and came rushing to our house because he thought his daughter would be with my mother—as I said, my mother often kept the child while Mrs. Galworthy was out."

"But the little girl wasn't there?"

"No, she wasn't. Mrs. Galworthy had telephoned that afternoon, you see . . . oh yes, the Galworthys and the Hootons were some of the first in Garnet to get telephones installed, my dear. My family was rather well off in those days. That was, of course, before the stock market crash of '29 . . . and as you know, our house is the museum now . . ." Her voice trailed off.

Miranda steered her gently back on course. "The little girl's mother called?"

"Yes." Mrs. Wainwright adjusted her scarf and swirled the tea in her glass. "Mrs. Galworthy decided at the last minute to take the child with her, and so they were both killed. That's the real tragedy, you see. The dear mother only wanted to give her daughter a nice day's outing in the city, and it ended in both their deaths. Fate can be so cruel." She stood up. "But it was all a long time ago, dear. It has nothing to do with you."

"Well, they lived in my house."

"But after Sigmund Galworthy moved away, no one lived in your house until the Kramers moved in. A long, long time later. You see, after Mr. Galworthy came to our house to collect the child and found she had gone with his wife, he was inconsolable. My father drove him back to identify her body ... it must have been awful. Fire had broken out on the train after the crash, and everyone was badly burned. Some of the bodies weren't identifiable at all. My father brought Mr. Galworthy back to our house to stay with us until he felt better. Only he didn't get better — he stayed in bed for weeks and weeks and lost interest in everything. When he finally did go back across the street, it was only to collect some clothes and important papers; he didn't stay. I guess living there would have always reminded him of what he'd lost. So he left everything and boarded up the house right after the funeral. People always wondered why he didn't just sell it. But then years later the Kramers moved in. Andrew Kramer was a nephew, I believe. He inherited the house but, as I told you, didn't end up staying long.

"I heard some talk about Sigmund Galworthy's will. Apparently Andrew Kramer couldn't sell the house; he had to leave it to his children. When he died, the house went to those boys; only it seems *they* weren't bound by the will, because they put the house up for sale immediately. And now you folks have it!" She beamed at Miranda. "Quite a story, isn't it?"

Miranda digested what Mrs. Wainwright told her with a sense of wonderment. Andrew *dead?* "How did Andrew Kramer die, do you know?"

"Goodness, child! I expect it was old age. We all have to go sometime." She finished her tea. "Lordy! Look at the clock! I must give you your lesson before my last pupil comes. Gracious me, I never realized how time was flying. Once you get me started—"

"But—" Miranda didn't want this conversation to end. "About the fire?"

"My dear, all this happened a very long time ago. I don't know much more to tell! Oh, look, the ice in your tea is all melted. Do you want to finish it, or should I throw it out?"

"I—uh, I had enough, thanks," Miranda replied.

Mrs. Wainwright poured the nearly full glass of tea down the drain, then wiped her hands on her skirt. "We can talk again," she promised. "I can tell you the history of nearly every family in town! Seems you're a regular little historian yourself. Must take after your father. I hear he teaches American history. Or used to. Maybe he'll give a lecture for us some evening. And we'll get you joining the Ladies' Guild someday, how will that be?"

"I'd like to hear more about my house," said Miranda, picking up her flute and music books.

Mrs. Wainwright motioned her into the sun-filled music room. "Patience, patience, my girl. Anything I can tell you about your house happened long before you were born. Let's deal with the present before we tackle the past. The present is your flute lesson, and that's what matters now."

# 9

Dinner that evening was another subdued meal. Miranda felt her mother glancing at her as she ate, but she kept her own eyes averted and finished her food quickly. After dinner, as usual, she climbed the stairs into the hot stuffy attic, opened the low windows, and turned on the fan. Settling herself comfortably behind the house, she folded her arms on the ledge of the dollhouse attic floor and peered through the windows. The attic she saw was the Kramers', black-curtained and empty. She waited but nothing happened. No one came upstairs after nearly ten minutes of waiting, so she lowered herself to a somewhat less comfortable position at the second-story level and looked out the windows of her miniature bedroom. There she found Timothy Kramer's bed unmade and his school clothes tossed carelessly on the floor. Jeff's side of the room was no neater. She went from room to room, peering through the windows. Nothing. Maybe no one was home. But when she came to the living room she drew closer with an exclamation of surprise and pleasure. This was not the Kramers' living room; it was a room from the past she had never seen before.

A fire burned in the grate and a man sat quietly with his legs stretched out in front of him and a newspaper lying unread across the bulk of his stomach, his eyes steadily watching the darting flames. Miranda decided that, from the look of his clothes and the room's furnishings, he must belong to the 1904 house. The furniture was heavy and dark, and portraits of whiskered men lined the wall above the rolltop desk. A mauve love seat hung with shiny tassles crouched in the far corner of the room. To the left of the love seat, a tall Christmas tree drooped, its red bows limp and faded. Dry pine needles littered the carpet around the tree, and one of the crimson candles had fallen from its holder and lay nestled among the branches near the bottom of the tree.

She was hardly surprised by the small, sickening lurch of terror that hit her. The terror always seemed to be present in 1904. But Miranda had learned that the terror *was* controllable. It had to do with holding in her stomach muscles and not breathing, clenching her fists and staring straight at the scene. By facing the terror this way, she was learning to conquer it.

And so she tightened her stomach and stared at the Christmas tree with stern control. Just as the terror subsided, Lucinda entered the room. She wore a shimmery dark blue gown, the waist very narrow. Silvery blue lace frothed around her throat and at her wrists. She stepped into the room without a sound, her magnolia scent overpowering the aroma of the pine Christmas tree.

The smell of magnolia set the terror churning again in Miranda's stomach, and she fought to ignore it. Lucinda walked over to the man and stood by his chair.

"Sigmund." Her voice rang sharply in the warm stillness of the room.

The man raised his eyes wearily and turned away from the flames to focus on her. "Yes, dear?"

"Don't you 'yes, dear' me!" She mimicked his belabored voice angrily.

"What is it, Lucinda?"

"You know perfectly well what it is! We haven't finished talking. How in the world am I to manage without the servants? I simply cannot! I won't have any time at all for my own pursuits."

"Lucinda, you know I wouldn't have let them go if there were any way to keep them. But we don't need so many servants! We can't afford to pay them! You've still got Hannah to help with Dorothy, and there's Mrs. Bowen."

"Bowen has quit! She left this afternoon when she heard that Mariette and Lizzie and Robert and Sam were all going."

"I'm sorry, Lucinda. We'll see if we can afford another cook. But you're going to need to help out, you know, by taking an interest yourself."

Lucinda hung on his arm. "I can help out much better than that, and you know it, Sigmund. I shall go out to work myself."

"Nonsense! No wife of mine works outside the home! And what could you do? Work in a shop, I suppose?" His voice was lightly scornful.

"Damnation! Sigmund, you *know* what I want to do. I've told you a hundred times I have no interest in housework or children — or shopkeeping! I want to be a lawyer, or else work in business."

He laughed. "And I've told you a hundred times that your interests are unnatural. Women aren't lawyers, Lucinda. The gentler sex simply isn't fit for the courtroom. Nor do they work well in offices."

"I don't know that *you're* so well fit for the courtroom yourself, Sigmund! If you'd only argued this last case the way I told you to, you wouldn't have lost!"

"My dear." Now his voice was cold. "That I lost a case has nothing whatever to do with the issue at hand."

"It does, Sigmund. It does!" Her beautiful face was suffused with scarlet. "I could have done a better job!"

He laughed. "You could do a better job here, my love, if you would attend to your duties. Dorothy is your job. And running the house. We simply can't afford to have a pack of servants doing work that is rightfully yours. The Galworthy women have lived here for generations without maids stationed in every room. And they were perfectly content with their lot!"

"They must have had brains of suet, but I certainly don't."

"Lucinda, you are being childish." He picked up the newspaper and rustled it. "Now, please. Let us have an end to this interview."

Lucinda whirled on him as swiftly as a cat. "If you loved me — no, not even that! If you were a decent man — you would see that I can't ever be happy like this. I told you before we married that I needed freedom. And you promised I'd have it! But I won't have any at all if we don't have servants."

"You have a lot more freedom than most women!" He peered over his paper. "You can buy jewels and clothes. You go out to the theater, traveling ... Most women in town envy you. And they manage quite well with one or two maids. Now, please. You tire me with your whining."

Lucinda clenched her hands in her skirts. "You're trying to keep me under your thumb! You think you own me! You try to stifle me, try to hold me down — but I won't let you. You can't keep me here! I am not your chattel!"

"Be silent, Lucinda! I've had quite enough of your hysterics."

She stormed to the door, almost colliding with a young woman dressed in gray. The girl stepped quickly aside, bobbing her head. Lucinda ignored her.

She turned back to stare at her husband. "You will have cause to remember this conversation, Sigmund." Then she swept past the girl, who sidled into the room and stood demurely until Sigmund Galworthy noticed her.

He sighed and lowered the newspaper. "What is it, Hannah?"

"It's Miss Dorothy, sir."

"What's wrong?"

"She won't eat her dinner, sir."

"My dear Hannah!" He came to stand beside her. "We have enough trouble just now without having to worry about whether Dorothy cleans her plate or not. Don't take it upon yourself." He turned away, dismissing her.

"Oh, but Mr. Galworthy!" Hannah boldly remained before him, and Sigmund turned back in surprise.

"Excuse me, but Mrs. Galworthy ordered me to make Miss Dorothy eat every last bit. Including the tomatoes, sir, and you know Miss Dorothy can't eat tomatoes. You know how sick she gets whenever she eats them . . . and I've tried, sir. I've been trying to get her to eat for the last hour, but she just can't."

"Look here, Hannah. Your job is to take care of Dorothy and so save me from scenes over tomatoes. Now go up and calm the child, and throw the damn — excuse me — throw the tomatoes in the garbage. Forget it. I don't want to hear any more about it."

"Oh, thank you, sir," cried Hannah with great relief, bobbing up and down respectfully. "But what about Mrs. Galworthy? She said earlier that the child was to clean her whole plate."

"My wife knows perfectly well that Dorothy can't stomach tomatoes. I will speak to her, Hannah." He removed a pipe from his vest pocket and polished its smooth bowl against his gray-trousered hip. "Now, unless there's something else you would like to discuss with me . . ."

"No, sir, thank you very much." She bobbed herself out of the room.

Miranda watched for a few more minutes, hoping something else would happen. Sigmund returned to his armchair in front of the fire. A small shower of sparks flew up the chimney. He stoked his pipe. Miranda had just started to turn away, not liking the strong odor of his pipe, when Dorothy appeared in the doorway.

She wore a long white flannel nightgown and her hair was tied back tightly in two long braids. She crept quietly over to Sigmund's chair and paused behind it. He sat once again gazing dreamily into the fire, puffing his pipe. Her small hands darted around and covered his eyes. "Guess who?" she said in a gruff voice.

"Oh my," said Sigmund mildly. "Is it Mr. Beecham from the office?"

Dorothy giggled, then quickly resumed the gruff tone. "No! Guess again."

"Is it Mrs. Hooton?"

"She doesn't have a voice like this!"

"*Mr.* Hooton, then?"

"No!"

"I shall never guess," moaned her father, and he reached his big hands over his head and down to close around her little body. He held her around the waist and hoisted her off the floor, tumbling her head-over-heels through the air above his head and down into his lap. Her laughter filled the room.

"Aha! Now I see it is only my little mouse."

Dorothy nestled against his chest. "I've come to say good night."

"I'm glad." He stroked the top of her head and fingered one of the long braids. "Do you know what the train conductor says when he blows the whistle?"

"What?"

"He says, 'Whooo-whooo!'" whistled Sigmund Galworthy, tugging on the braid as if pulling the chain on a train whistle.

They were still laughing together when Lucinda stalked into the room. "Dorothy! Hannah is looking for you! Get back upstairs and finish those tomatoes. And if you can't finish them before bedtime, you will see them in the morning for your breakfast."

Sigmund Galworthy set Dorothy back on her feet. "Dorothy will have an egg for breakfast," he said. "You know she can't eat tomatoes, Lucinda."

"The child must learn to eat what is set before her."

"That's enough. The subject is closed. Dorothy will have the same food for breakfast as you and I do."

Lucinda pulled herself up majestically. "Mister Galworthy," she began bitingly, "you have already deprived me of my staff. If I'm in charge of the house, then I shall run it *my* way. If you don't like the way things are run here"—her voice rose dramatically—"then you might think about living elsewhere!"

Sigmund faced her, calmly. "That is enough shouting." His voice was soft, but as icy as her own. Dorothy edged behind her father. "I shall take Dorothy up to bed myself, Lucinda, and I will thank you to retire immediately. You will kindly remember that in this house you do not raise your voice to me. Is that clear?"

Lucinda glared at him. "Perhaps you would like *me* to live elsewhere?"

"Don't be absurd. You are my wife. Now go up to bed. I'm sick and tired of your theatrics."

She leveled a bitter stare at him and swung on her heel, leaving the room. Dorothy began to whimper, holding onto her father's leg. Sigmund picked her up and held her tightly against him for a moment. Then he set her down.

"There, there, little mouse. Mama and Daddy are just a little angry now, but everything will be better tomorrow. Come on, now. I'll take you up to Hannah." He reached for her hand.

Dorothy hung back. Her eyes were dark and clouded. Sigmund smiled down at her and touched the tip of her pert nose with a long finger. He reached for a braid and tugged it. "Someday I'm going to cut off one of these and use it for a paintbrush, old girl. What do you say to that?"

Miranda smiled at this weak attempt to cheer up the little girl, but Dorothy wrapped her arms around him fiercely. "Daddy," she murmured, "is Mama going away?"

"Your Mama is just upset tonight, sweetheart. She's not leaving."

She hugged him more tightly. "But Daddy, don't *you* ever go away!"

"No one is going away, darling."

She pushed her face into his lap. When she spoke again, her voice was muffled. "Daddy, promise? Daddy—will you be here when I wake up?"

Sigmund rested his hand on her soft hair and gazed at the flames for a long moment without seeming to see them. Then, "Yes," he said. "Yes, Mouse. I'll be here. Always."

Miranda closed her eyes. This had already happened. But when? Where?

When she opened her eyes again, the Galworthys' living room was empty. Dorothy's sad little question hung in the air. "Will you be here when I wake up?"

Where had Miranda heard that before?

It hit her suddenly. Of course! Timmy Kramer had asked his parents that question, the night Iris tried to hit him with a lamp. In fact, hadn't she herself asked her parents that same thing only a week or two ago? She remembered feeling silly after asking it, because of course her parents would be there in the morning. Why had she asked the question at all?

Miranda sat back on her heels. An idea was beginning to form in her head. What if—what if she and Timmy had only asked the question because Dorothy asked it years earlier? Could that be?

Miranda shivered in the warm attic. Watching through the dollhouse windows was natural to her now. But the past was past. It had to be. The thought that the lives of prior occupants of the house could touch her own, however briefly, struck chords of fear in Miranda.

The Kramers certainly seemed ordinary enough. But the Galworthys, Sigmund and Lucinda, were weird. Miranda didn't quite understand what the trouble was. It sounded as if Lucinda wanted a career and Sigmund said she couldn't have one—what a chauvinist! But it also sounded as if Lucinda was a pretty bad mother. Imagine trying to force a little girl to eat leftover tomatoes, which made her sick, for breakfast if she left them on her plate at dinner! That was plain cruelty. Not that Miranda herself had anything against tomatoes, but if, for instance, the food had been liver —

Wait a minute. *Tomatoes?* Hadn't Helen said something odd about tomatoes recently? Yes — while making cheese sandwiches: "I've burned yours, Mandy."

"Mine? Do I get a special one?"

"Yours doesn't have any tomatoes, of course. You've always hated tomatoes . . ."

But it wasn't Miranda who hated tomatoes.

Miranda shook her head as if to clear it. From downstairs in her parents' bedroom the voices of Helen and Philip, raised in yet another quarrel, reached her ears.

# 10

Back in her bedroom, Miranda sat on the window seat and stared down at the tangled front lawn. Dusk settled slowly, whispering through the pines that surrounded the house. She could see the dark branches of the magnolia tree twisting in the light wind, and she felt as unsettled as they were. She was on edge and needed to calm down. Music would help. Music always helped. It had been a while since she played her flute just for the joy of playing. Lessons were one thing, but the notes that flew into the air when she played out of a private need were clearer and more lilting; a lullaby to herself.

She opened her closet and pulled out the flute case. She carried the case over to the window seat and began fitting the instrument together automatically. Not bothering to set up her music stand, she stood at the window and held the flute to her lips.

But as Miranda stared out at the trees, no music came. She couldn't think what to play. She paused, licked her lips, and tried again. She blew softly, pressing her fingers on the silver keys. A thread of a tune moved through her bedroom. She sang the words in her head:

> *Golden slumbers fill your eyes*
> *While overhead the stars arise.*
> *Sleep pretty baby, do not cry,*
> *And I will sing a lullaby . . .*

She saw in her mind Dorothy's golden hair. Who had ever sung lullabies to Dorothy? Sigmund? Maybe Hannah? Miranda sighed and stopped playing. The music wasn't helping her tonight.

Thoughts clamored in Miranda's head — each needing to be pondered separately, each important as part of a whole that was not yet clear to her. Fragments of words she had heard and things she had seen in the dollhouse nudged her memory insistently, urging her to sort them out.

She laid her flute abruptly on the seat cushion and crossed to her bookshelf, where she unearthed *Garnet Township in the Nineteenth Century* from beneath a pile of music sheets. She sat cross-legged on the floor, turning the pages of Mrs. Wainwright's slim green book. At the open window, the curtains stirred in a sudden, welcome gust of wind.

Miranda studied each page carefully, not knowing what she was looking for, but certain of recognizing it when she saw it. The book was an account of the social and political life of Garnet over the last century. Miranda flipped past descriptions of pre–Civil War balls hosted by the wealthy who summered in Garnet to escape the heat of Boston and New York. She was interested in more recent history. As she skimmed the chapter covering the abolitionist movement in Garnet, a familiar name leaped off the page at her from the section about the Underground Railroad: Hooton.

With growing interest, she read how the Hooton family in the mid-nineteenth century hid runaway slaves in a secret cupboard behind the cellar stairs until the Southern slave-catchers gave up searching for them and returned to the South.

She skipped the next few pages, uninterested in farm reports and the political scandal of 1880, when the elderly mayor of Garnet married a local girl who was only sixteen. Near the end of the book she found a section on the population growth in Garnet, including a list of the inhabitants in 1800 and another of the inhabitants in 1900. The Hooton and Galworthy families were listed in both, but it was in the list for 1900 that Miranda finally found what she was looking for:

GALWORTHY, Sigmund E., Attorney-at-Law
Wife: Lucinda Walker Galworthy
Children: Dorothy Arabella Galworthy

Miranda closed the book, trying to bring order to her tumbling thoughts. The information in the book only confirmed what Mrs. Wainwright had told her, but seeing the names of her dollhouse ghosts in print left Miranda with a creepy feeling.

She flopped onto her back and stared up at the ceiling. She could hardly see into the corners because the room had grown dark while she sat deep in thought. She heard footsteps climbing the attic stairs and then coming down again. Her father's voice called to her.

"I'm in here," she said, her voice flat and loud in the dim quiet of her bedroom.

Philip appeared in the doorway, Helen behind him. "Oh, there you are," he said. "I thought you'd be up in the attic." He did not add "as usual," but Miranda knew he was thinking it.

"No, I've been here," she said, sitting up. "Reading."

"In this light?" Helen pushed past Philip into the room.

"Well, it only just got dark."

Philip looked down at the green book on the floor. "What were you reading?"

Miranda reached over and handed it to him. "Mrs. Wainwright, my flute teacher, wrote it. She's historian of the Ladies' Guild."

"Ah," said Philip, leafing through the volume. "Is it interesting?"

"It's okay." She was noncommittal.

All three waited, uncomfortable around each other, not knowing what to say. The memory of the awful scene in the car still hung heavy in the muggy air. No one knew quite how to erase it.

"Well, I'm off to bed," Helen announced.

"Good night," mumbled Miranda.

"Good night, Helen," said Philip.

She left the room and Philip stared after her for a long moment. Then he looked down at Miranda. "Do you like it here?"

"It's okay."

"You wouldn't want to move?"

"No!" She tried to see his face in the dark room, but couldn't. She got up and turned on her desk light. "Why? Don't you like it here anymore?"

"I like it here very much."

"Then what's this about moving?"

"It's important to me that we can all be happy here. And right now we aren't a very merry group, I'd say."

Miranda considered this. "True. But I don't see how moving would help anything. It probably takes time to get used to a new place." She felt very mature saying that. "After all, we haven't been here long."

Philip smiled at her. "Good for you, honey!" Then he sighed. "But your mother wants to move — not back to New York, but to another house in Garnet."

Immediately the thought darted into her head: if they had to move, could she take the dollhouse along? She'd have to! "Dad, this house is the best part about living here!"

"I agree, Mandy. I'm hoping for a lot this year, now that I've got my health back. I'm trying to figure out what I want to do with my life — professionally, that is. I know I don't want to teach anymore. Fixing up this house is more or less therapy for me! It helps me think. But your mother is unhappy. She doesn't like the house anymore — we've been, ah, *discussing* it."

"So I heard." She searched his face. "Oh, Dad, what doesn't she like? What can we *do?*"

"In answer to both those questions — I'm not sure. It's a puzzle to me. She's become very moody. It's un-

like her, but there you are. If it were you, we'd probably say it was just a stage! Maybe that's what Mither is
going through." His arms closed around her in a big
hug, and he spoke quietly. "But she'll come out of it.
We'll be okay. Don't worry, little mouse." And then he
was gone, shutting the bedroom door softly.

Little mouse?

So she wasn't crazy, and she wasn't imagining
things. And it wasn't just the dollhouse that showed
her the past. She saw it happening right here in her
own house, like repeat performances of very old plays.
A drama played out in three different times with three
different casts, yet the same story unfolding in each,
the same lines being spoken.

But who had written the script? And how did the
story end?

# 11

Miranda awoke early the next morning when a clap of thunder shook the house and a strong gust of wind rattled the shade of the lamp on her bed-side table. She sat up, confused. A golden glow filled the sky outside the window.

A New England summer storm was brewing, but to Miranda, accustomed to the dreary patter of gray city showers, the golden light and howling wind seemed to come from another world. Her alarm clock read 6:15 — too early for her parents to be up. She stood by her window seat, looking out at the branches whip-ping the leaves of the magnolia tree back and forth. Then she slid the windows shut. She crept out into the hall past her parents' door and listened. Apparently they slept on, undisturbed by the storm. She slipped downstairs, her hand sliding over the smooth wooden banister as little Dorothy's hand, Lucinda's hand, and Sigmund's hand had done so long ago. Had the Kra-mer boys tried sitting at the top and sliding down the curve to the hallway below? Probably.

In the kitchen she poured herself a glass of milk and slid a piece of blueberry pie—left over from last night's dessert—onto a plate. She carried these carefully back up the stairs and then up the narrower, shadowy climb to the attic. Settled on the pillows behind the dollhouse, she ate her breakfast and waited. Outside, the treetops waved back and forth, creaking in the gale. The windowpanes rattled.

Suddenly the wind stopped, the trees became still, and the world seemed to pause. It was unnaturally quiet. Miranda set her plate on the floor and walked over to the windows. A quick volley of thunder burst forth like a series of gunshots. She drew back just as the rain, sounding like tennis balls on the roof, hurtled down.

A light spray gusted in through the windows. Miranda hastily closed them, but then opened them again, as the room immediately seemed too stuffy. She knew that rainstorms usually broke the heat and humidity, but this storm was doing nothing to make the attic more bearable. She returned to the dollhouse, finishing off the last bites of pie before ducking her head to see what was happening this morning.

It was midday on an autumn afternoon and Iris Kramer stood at the kitchen counter making bacon, lettuce, and tomato sandwiches for lunch. She hummed as she removed the bacon from the frying pan and arranged it on the toasted slices of bread. The two small Kramer boys tumbled through the back door, their cheeks rosy from the brisk autumn air.

"Guess what, Mommy!"

"Let me tell! We saw—"

"I'm telling! I saw him first!"

"Boys!" The welcoming smile faded from her lips. "First get your coats off. And your hands need washing."

Soon the boys were seated and vying for her attention again. Their voices rose. "The Hootons have a dog, Mommy!" Jeff said excitedly.

"It's Eddie Hooton's new dog!"

"A big, shaggy black one, and he's only a puppy and he'll get lots bigger! Hey, can we have a dog?"

"Yeah, Mom, we want a dog, too!"

Iris leaned against the stove and wiped her hands on a towel, her forehead creased in a frown.

"Mom? Can we? Can we?"

"Oh please, oh please, Mommy?"

"No dog," she told them. "Who would end up feeding it? And housebreaking it? And keeping its paws off the furniture? And what about taking it for walks?"

"But Mom! It would be so great! We'd take care of it ourselves. You wouldn't have to do anything, honest!"

"Only very good boys get dogs. Now eat your lunches and go outside to play. I have a headache."

Iris always had headaches, reflected Miranda. Some of them were so bad that she had to lie down in a dark room with a compress on her forehead. When Miranda settled down to watch through the dollhouse windows she would encounter Iris again and again, lying down in various rooms with a cool compress on

her forehead. And once or twice Miranda had seen Lucinda Galworthy in bed in a darkened room, with
Hannah hovering over her. The maid had urged Lucinda to sip from a glass of water mixed with something Hannah called a "headache powder."

"We're good boys!" said Jeff.

"We won't say a single word," vowed Timmy.

"You won't even know we're here," cried Jeff, "because we'll be quiet as a mouse."

"As a *dog,* not a mouse!" shrieked Timmy with glee.

Iris put her hands to her head. "Boys!" They qui-
eted instantly. "Not another word out of either of you."
She looked momentarily surprised at the cold rage in
her tone. Their silence lasted but a few seconds, then
was broken by Timmy's sullen voice.

"*Yuck.* You put *tomatoes* in here." He threw down
the offending sandwich.

"Of course I did, Timothy Kramer," she snapped.
"Bacon, lettuce, and tomato sandwiches always have
tomatoes in them. Now *eat.*"

"I *hate* tomatoes!"

"Since when?" Iris flew from the stove, brandishing
a wooden spoon. "Just be quiet and eat them!" she
screamed, reaching for Timmy. He dodged her grasp
and ran from the room.

"I said be *quiet!*" She lunged for the sobbing Jeff,
but he, too, ran from the room. Iris stood there at the
table, smacking her hand with the spoon, her face a
mask of dark fury.

Miranda backed away from the dollhouse, looking
up into her own attic as a clap of thunder rattled the

121

windowpanes and shook the walls. Rain sprayed through the open windows, and Miranda jumped up to close them.

Angry torrents slashed the house, and winds tore small branches from the trees. She sat back down against the wall, her eyes closed. She hardly noticed the storm; her mind was busy trying to grasp the elusive memory that threatened to disappear the way dreams do upon awakening.

She was trembling, suddenly afraid but unable to pinpoint the fear. It had something to do with waiting—as if she were waiting for something to happen. She opened her eyes and ran downstairs.

Helen was still in bed when Miranda peered into the darkened bedroom.

"I'm sick," her mother said peevishly. "It's a gruesome day and I have a horrible headache."

"Can I get you some aspirin?"

"No." Helen pulled the sheet up to her chin and turned onto her side. "It's still raining."

Miranda walked to the window and drew back the curtain. "But not quite as hard as before."

"Oh, I can't bear it. This is awful. We never had weather like this in New York."

"Oh, come on, Mither! Don't you remember the power failure after that huge storm last year—and the elevators didn't work and Mrs. Rosenbaum got stuck and almost had her baby right there?"

Helen closed her eyes, and her lips hardened into a stern line. "I have a headache, Miranda."

*"Sorry!"* Miranda left the room, resisting the impulse to slam the door behind her. She trudged into her room and threw herself down onto her window seat, where she peered gloomily out at the rain. She watched two fat raindrops race each other down the pane. The one on the right seemed to be winning, but as Miranda watched, a gust of wind blew the drop on the left into its path, and the two droplets merged and slid down as one onto the windowsill.

She soon found herself, oddly, near tears. There was something about rain that made her feel lonely. She never felt like this on sunny days. But today she felt just like one of the raindrops, sliding down a path not of her own choosing, forced on by a storm raging all around her. She wished that she, like the raindrops on the windowpane, could melt into someone else, find someone to share the dollhouse compulsion and terror.

Miranda raised her eyes and stared out at the lights shining in the Hootons' house across the street. They seemed to beckon to her.

*I suppose I could go visit,* she thought. She tugged a brush through her hair and went down to the kitchen to tell her father where she was going. The screen door slammed behind her as she ran out of the house, and Miranda heard Helen's voice all the way from the bedroom: "Can't that girl be *quiet?*"

Miranda paused a moment on the porch steps to open her umbrella, and ended up scrambling after it across the wild front garden as the wind whipped it off on a journey of its own.

Light shone out through the stained glass window of the Hootons' front door as Buddy opened it with a big smile. "Oh, good!" he said. "Come on in!"

"Hi." She stood with her bare arms held out stiffly from her sides as water droplets ran down them. "I've come to visit," she added, unnecessarily.

"And we're glad," said Virginia Hooton, entering the shadowy hallway from a door leading off into a room on the left. Her friendly face was all smiles. "Come get dried off."

She shook the water from Miranda's umbrella, then left it in the foyer to dry. Miranda was led into a cheerful dining room. The polished round table was laden with teacups and a plate of coffee cake. A huge bowl of pink roses dominated the center of the table. Dan, Mr. Hooton, and Mrs. Wainwright sat munching coffee cake and talking.

"Morning," mumbled Mr. Hooton, his mouth full.

"Miranda dear," exclaimed Mrs. Wainwright. "A lovely surprise!"

"Hello!" Miranda paused and looked at Mr. Hooton. "I didn't know you had company already . . ."

"Aunt Ellie wouldn't thank me to call her company," he smiled, wiping crumbs from his lip with a napkin.

"I should say not," said Mrs. Wainwright. "Have a seat, dear."

Mrs. Hooton offered tea, which Miranda declined, but she did accept a cup of hot chocolate and a towel to dry her hair and arms. She sat next to Dan, who raised an eyebrow at her. His expression was dour. She raised her brows back at him.

"Glad you could tear yourself away from your house," he said, as he passed her the coffee cake. Miranda selected a small piece. "We never thought we'd actually get the legendary Miranda Browne into our humble dwelling."

Mrs. Hooton smiled. "Dan's a tease," she said. Miranda would have called him sarcastic and rude, if anyone had asked her honest opinion.

She didn't bother to look at Dan Hooton again but passed the plate on to Mr. Hooton. "Is this your breakfast?" she asked.

"No, we ate hours ago," Mr. Hooton told her. "Everyone is up early around here. This is just a snack to tide us over till lunch."

"We eat a lot," added Buddy, helping himself to another piece of coffee cake.

Mrs. Wainwright nodded approvingly. "With two healthy boys in the house, you've got to have a lot of food on hand." She smiled at Miranda. "You look like you could use a little fattening up yourself, dear."

"Here, Skinny," said Buddy, passing her another piece of coffee cake.

"Slender," corrected Dan. Miranda looked up, startled, to find him smiling at her. His smile transformed his whole face. Was he a jerk or wasn't he? She felt confused and changed the subject.

"I've been reading your book," she told Mrs. Wainwright. "I found it in the library. It's really interesting."

"Thank you! I'm planning to write a history of the Hooton family next." She sipped her coffee. "In between music students."

"Oh, yes! I forgot you were a Hooton, too."

"Bite your tongue," chided Dan. "Once a Hooton, always a Hooton."

"Every Hooton for the last two hundred years has lived in this house for some time at least," said Mrs. Wainwright. "Any story of the family would also be a story of the house. My great-grandfather and grandfather and father were all born right upstairs, just as I was myself."

"And you, too—right, Dad?" asked Buddy.

"Well, no. I was born in the Garnet Hospital," he admitted. "Times change."

"Tell us how it was in the old days, Aunt El." Buddy twinkled at her across the table. "When you were a girl."

"Old days!" Mrs. Wainwright pursed her lips. "I'm sure when we were busy living them we never thought they'd come to be called the old days! You just wait, Buddy. Wait till you're an old man and your grandchildren ask you about the old days when you sat gobbling coffee cake during a storm."

Buddy considered this. "But this is *now*," he said. "*Now* can't be called the old days!"

His mother reached over and ruffled his hair. "Oh, Buddy, eight years old is too young to start thinking about the vagaries of time."

Mrs. Wainwright spread jam on a thick slice of bread. "Nonsense. He lives in a museum. Everything is a matter of time. The present becomes both past and future — depending which way you look at it."

"Sure," said Dan. "We can say 'tomorrow is Monday,' but then tomorrow we'll say '*today* is Monday,' and then on Tuesday we'll say, '*yesterday* was Monday,' so Monday exists in the past, present, *and* future! It depends on which point of view you take."

Miranda thought about her dollhouse. "But do you think it's possible for times to exist at the same time? I mean, I know it sounds crazy, but do you think it would be possible for times to sort of overlap?"

"Sounds like science fiction to me," said Dan.

"But the idea is fascinating," said Mrs. Hooton. "I've always wished that time machines existed — I'd love to travel back in time."

"I'd go back to see the cowboys," said Buddy.

"I think I'd go some place really interesting," mused Mrs. Wainwright. "Or should I say some *time* really interesting? Medieval England!"

"What about you, Mandy?" asked Mr. Hooton. "Where would you go?"

"Oh, I don't know. I was wondering more if it would be possible to *see* into other times — not actually travel back to them and walk around, but just be able to *watch*."

"Like a fly on the wall, huh?" asked Dan. "You're there and nobody knows it. Peeping Mandy!"

"Something like that," replied Miranda, refusing to laugh with him. She hesitated. "Like looking through a window into another time, for example."

Mr. Hooton nodded. "But how would it work?

Would you be watching time unfold as it happens — or would you just be watching it as if it were a film, similar to television? Would the past be broadcast live or pre-recorded?"

"An interesting question, Ed," agreed Mrs. Wainwright. "And living here in Garnet gives one a special feel for the past, I think. United States history begins in this area."

"Think of the history this house alone has seen!" marveled Mrs. Hooton. "The Revolutionary War, the Civil War... In fact, caring about time is really what led us to turn this place into a museum. Right, Ed? Caring about the past enough to spend the present guarding it for the future."

"A tough job!" cried Mr. Hooton, rather dramatically. "But somebody's got to do it!"

They all laughed. Buddy grabbed the last piece of coffee cake.

"Our house was part of the Underground Railroad," Dan told Miranda. "Did you know that? It was probably the most important job this old house ever had."

"You mean *trains* came through our house?" asked Buddy, quite confused. "But the train station isn't even close by!"

"No," Dan explained through their laughter. "The Underground Railroad was just a name for the chain of families who helped slaves escape from the Southern states to the North and Canada. The slaves had to have somewhere safe to hide until they could get to freedom."

"We learned about that in school last year," said Miranda. "It was very dangerous for the runaways, but also for the people who helped them escape, because that was against the law."

"Dan and Buddy will have to show you the secret room," said Mrs. Wainwright. "When my brothers and I were little we used to play there. One of us played the runaway slave, and the others were the slave-catcher and the person hiding the slave." She grimaced. "I was the youngest and had to be the slave most of the time. It was terrible."

"But you can bet it was more terrible actually *being* a slave," said Mr. Hooton.

"Of course, Ed! But you know what I mean. Didn't you play in the room when you were a boy? You know it was much more fun to be the slave-catcher asking questions or the owner of the house making up lies to keep the slave safe, than to hide in the dark behind the false wall."

"False wall!" cried Miranda. "This I've got to see."

"It's wild," Dan said. "The whole back wall under the basement stairs slides away—but you'd never know it. It's almost impossible to detect cracks in the stone." With his face flushed and animated, he no longer looked the slightest bit dour. "The Hootons who lived here then—I mean in the years before the Civil War—built the secret space themselves. They couldn't even trust outside carpenters to come in."

"As far as we know, the Galworthy and Hooton men did all the work themselves," added his mother.

"Galworthy?" exclaimed Miranda. "Does that mean

our house might have been a stop on the Underground Railroad, too?"

"Indeed it was!" said Mrs. Wainwright. She sat back in her chair abruptly. "Don't tell me you haven't found the secret room yet!"

# 12

Miranda actually dropped her fork. Everyone laughed at her dramatic response, Mrs. Wainwright loudest of all.

"My goodness!" She adjusted one of her colorful scarves. "How awful to be living in a house with a secret hiding place and not even know it."

"But where is it?" asked Miranda.

"I don't know—I've never seen it," said Mrs. Wainwright. "But I do know the story behind it."

Miranda sat back in her chair and stared across the table expectantly. She could see the branches of trees outside the window slashing back and forth in the wind and could hear the muted gush of rain pouring from the gutters. She waited for Mrs. Wainwright's story with a thrill of excitement. These new revelations about her house could only add to the magic it held for her already.

"Come on, Aunt El," Buddy urged. "It's story time!"

"She wants us to beg her," teased Dan. "Please tell? Pretty please?"

"You two just hush," replied the old woman. "Let me make sure I've got the facts straight."

Mr. Hooton poured her another cup of coffee. "Here, this will get the old story-telling juices flowing."

She sipped her coffee and patted her lips neatly with a napkin. Miranda felt ready to burst with waiting. Mrs. Wainwright finally cleared her throat.

"If I recall correctly," she began, "the hiding space in your house, Miranda dear, was built even before ours here. But there was a big problem with the Galworthys' secret room—one nobody found out about until the first family of slaves to hide there nearly suffocated after a few hours in the small space. The hiding place was airtight!"

"Were the people all right?" Miranda asked.

"They were unconscious, I believe. But the Galworthys were able to revive them. The fugitives stayed at the house a week to recuperate, and then the Galworthys helped them move on. I remember hearing that while they waited, the father of the escaping family, who was a carpenter, built a special dollhouse for the Galworthy children. He worked on it day and night—maybe to keep himself from worrying about the journey that lay ahead for him and his family. It was supposed to be a miniature of the big house—in every detail except for the hidden room."

She paused and sipped her coffee, looking around the table at her rapt audience. "Perhaps leaving out the secret room was his message to all the children who would play with the house—that houses shouldn't have to have secret rooms. That people shouldn't have to be on the run."

It was on the tip of Miranda's tongue to tell them she had found the dollhouse, but the same odd sense that she mustn't tell her parents about the magic kept her silent now.

"How did they fix the secret room?" she asked instead. "I mean so they could use it again. Did they just poke some airholes in it, or something?"

"No, they decided not to use the room again. They were afraid that any modifications that would make the room safe would also make it easier to detect."

"What about a hidden vent with a fan system or something?" asked Dan.

"We're talking mid-nineteenth century," his father reminded him.

"In any case," continued Mrs. Wainwright, "the Hootons were building their own hiding place, and by the time more slaves came along the Underground network, the room under the stairs here was ready."

"And we Hootons know how to build things right!" cried Buddy.

"Well," laughed Mrs. Wainwright, "*those* Hootons surely did. The Galworthy hiding place was never used as a stop on the Railroad again, as far as I know."

Miranda felt a surge of excitement start at her toes and move up through her whole body. She was tingling with the desire to jump up and run home to look for that airtight room.

"Want to see our secret hiding place?" Buddy asked, and she had to will herself to calm down.

"Sure," she said. "But then I'd better be getting home."

Dan squinted at her in such a way that she knew he was aware of her eagerness to be off. Well, so what?

Buddy scraped back his chair. "Come on! The tour starts here!"

"I'll come, too," said Dan, and he and Miranda followed Buddy.

They hurried through a large kitchen, into a narrow pantry, out again into a laundry room, where an ironing board piled high with rumpled shirts nearly capsized as they passed. Around a few more corners — then they stood before a low wooden door.

"The old cellar," Buddy announced.

"How many cellars do you have?"

"Two," answered Dan. "This old one, which isn't used anymore except when we take museum tours down to see the hiding place. And then there's one on the other side of the house — it's more a proper basement. That's where we keep all our junk."

Buddy led the way down the steep flight of narrow stairs. Dan followed, and Miranda came last. "Watch your head at the bottom," Dan turned to caution her. "The ceiling slopes low."

The cellar was cold and empty. The only light came from a ventilation slit up high by the ceiling, covered with a grate. It led directly outside. "This is where they stored meat and other food that had to stay cold," said Dan. "There were no lights down here — but darkness was to the slaves' advantage. It made it harder to see the cracks around the hidden door."

"Where *is* the door?" Miranda asked.

Buddy shrieked with laughter. "You're looking right at it!"

"But *where?*" She peered at the stone wall in front of her and then back at the boys.

"You'd make a terrible slave-catcher," said Dan.

"I take that as a compliment," she retorted.

"I meant it as one!" His hand brushed her shoulder. "Here, look."

He trailed one finger along the wall. As far as she could make out there was no crack, no indentation or marking to suggest a door. And yet under Dan's hand, an entire section of the wall slid sideways and a hole appeared, leading into the hidden chamber.

"That's incredible!" The tingle of excitement shot upwards again.

Buddy grabbed her hand. "Come on, I'll show you!"

Dan stood back and allowed Buddy and Miranda to enter the room. It was darker than any darkness Miranda had ever known. She couldn't see her hand in front of her eyes. "I can't believe this," she cried, groping with one arm for the walls. "It's pitch black!"

Dan shone a flashlight in from the entrance. "Let's shed a little light on the subject."

Now Miranda could see that the room was only about five feet square and furnished with two long wooden benches, a pile of gray woolen blankets, an earthenware jug, and a tin pail. The floor and walls were made of stone, and the cold was bone-chilling.

"Not a place you'd want to hang out in for long,"

Dan said lightly. "But it did its job well enough." He beamed the light onto the jug. "Mom set this stuff up in here to show how it looked back then. That jug was for drinking water. The pail was their toilet."

"When you gotta go, you gotta go," said Buddy.

"Yeah. They might have had to hide for hours at a time."

"Can you imagine how it must have been for those poor people, having to hide here?" asked Miranda, backing out of the cold little room. "God!" She had a glimmer of insight into the fascination history held for her father, whose interest in the past had always seemed inexplicable. She'd felt, when she thought about it at all, that the past had never been as alive as the present. Yet what she saw through the dollhouse was vivid, and this hiding place with its pile of blankets and jug for water was so real that for a moment time seemed to invert itself, and she thought for a second she heard the thump of a slave-catcher's boots on the narrow cellar steps.

"At least the slaves were safe here, even if they weren't very comfortable," said Dan, his voice pulling her back to the present. "Think how much worse it would have been to believe you were going to get help and then end up nearly dead in a room without air."

"You mean what happened in my house." She took a deep breath, knowing it was only in her imagination that the cold air in the cellar was too thin to fill her lungs. She inspected the sliding door hastily and saw that the stones were only a veneer cemented onto a wooden panel. Abruptly, she headed for the stairs. "Let's go."

"Yeah." Dan led the way back up the stairs and through the hallways to the dining room. "Want to start looking now?"

"For what?" But of course she knew.

"Your airtight room!"

"You mean you want to help me?" Miranda hesitated. She felt proprietary about her house and wanted to guard its secrets.

"What are we waiting around for?" cried Buddy.

"Miranda hasn't invited you," Dan told his brother. "She might not want a noisy, argumentative little boy invading her house."

Dan seemed oblivious to the fact that she hadn't invited him, either—but she didn't want to be rude.

"No, it's okay," she said. "You both can come."

Miranda said good-bye to Mr. and Mrs. Hooton and Mrs. Wainwright, and the boys told their parents the plan.

Mr. Hooton looked at his watch. "Sounds fine—but remember, Dan, you said you'd help me catalog the Revolutionary War maps this afternoon. Can you be back by two?"

Dan nodded. "I work in the museum on weekends," he told Miranda. "Earn my allowance."

"It's more than that," Mr. Hooton added. "I really need his help. There's a lot to do to keep this old place going."

"You can say that again!" said Dan. "But turning the

place into a museum was about the only way we could afford to keep it in the family."

"It's fascinating! My father would love to see the secret room."

"Any of you are welcome anytime for a private tour," said Mrs. Hooton. She handed Miranda her umbrella as they stepped out onto the porch.

Miranda and the boys dashed, rain hard on their backs, through her tangled garden and up onto the porch.

"It's really something to get a chance to see this house from the inside, you know," said Dan. "It's been shut up ever since my dad was a boy."

Miranda's father walked into the front hall from the dining room. "Hello! Is this a house-warming party?"

Miranda grabbed his arm. "We're on a treasure hunt! Did you know this house was part of the Underground Railroad before the Civil War?"

"Is that a fact? The house is certainly old enough to have been a stopping point."

"Mrs. Wainwright—she's the Hootons' aunt—said our house has a secret room!" She and Dan and Buddy recounted Mrs. Wainwright's tale.

"Quite a story! But where could the secret room be? I've been all over this place and never seen any sign of a hidden door." Philip looked puzzled.

"Well, that's what we're here for," said Buddy.

"If you don't mind," Dan amended.

"Of course I don't mind. Go right ahead and search. I'll help you myself, once I finish staining the book-cases in the library."

"I bet I find it myself," said Buddy. "I'm a good finder! I can find almost anything!"

"Yeah," said Dan. "Especially if it's something you're not supposed to have!"

Philip smiled at the boys. "Just make it a quiet search, please. Mandy, don't forget your mother is in bed." He walked back to the library, and Miranda and the boys went into the kitchen.

"Is your mother sick?" asked Dan.

"No, not really. Mither just has a headache or something."

"Mither?"

"It's a nickname I've had for her since I was small. My mother, Mom, whatever you want to call her — she never used to have headaches in New York, but it looks like Garnet isn't agreeing with her."

"Yeah," drawled Dan. "Must be hard being away from all that smog. Does your Dither get headaches, too?"

Miranda felt annoyed at his teasing. "Dad's fine," she said shortly. Then she pointed to the cellar door. "Look, we could start down there. Your secret room is in the cellar, so ours might be, too."

"Good idea," agreed Dan. "We'll start at the bottom of the house and work our way to the top."

The stone steps of the cellar were dark, lit only by a single bulb in a small cage hanging from the ceiling. It was not a large cellar, only half the size of the house, with damp gray walls and an uneven cement floor.

Miranda led the way down into the long, low room. One small window, high up on the end wall and covered by a grate, let in a narrow shaft of dim light. In a far corner stood a modern furnace and water heater.

"Check under the stairs first," said Dan. He started moving along the walls. "It's hard to be sure—sometimes the cracks are almost invisible."

Buddy explored the walls near the water heater. "Nothing back here but some boxes."

"We had the china packed in those." Miranda started wandering around the room, tapping occasionally on the stone walls.

Dan tiptoed up behind her, then suddenly clapped his hands onto her shoulders. "If that wall turns around suddenly and you disappear," he hissed into her ear, "don't say I didn't warn you!"

Miranda jumped. She could feel all of his fingers right through her T-shirt, ten warm points of contact. She turned around and he stepped back, letting his hands drop.

"Okay, let's stop, then," she said. "This looks to me like a good example of your basic bare room."

"But you're right to be tapping!" he said. "The hiding place wouldn't be much of a secret if we could spot it right away, would it? In fact, we should probably test all the walls to see if they're hollow." He reached over her head and rapped the wall with his knuckles. "If it sounds like that it's *not* hollow."

He was still standing very close, his arm raised, his eyes holding her own, and Miranda made no effort to move away. She forgot her earlier annoyance at his teasing and stared back at him. She hadn't noticed before how warm and brown his eyes were. Even in the gloom of the cellar, she could see the golden flecks of light in his irises. The tingle of excitement had started up in her again, but this time it had nothing to do with the past. She remembered the raindrops racing together down the pane.

"Both of your heads are hollow," commented Buddy pleasantly.

She laughed and ducked away under Dan's arm.

After twenty more minutes of tapping, they were convinced the cellar did not contain the secret room. They trooped upstairs and set off through the rooms on the ground floor, exploring each with the tapping technique. Their search revealed nothing. Undaunted, they set off for the second floor, but they were met at the top of the stairs by Philip, who shook his head.

"Sorry," he said in a subdued voice. "Mandy, your mother isn't feeling any better — I know she won't appreciate any tapping up here."

"Dad! We still have half the house to search!"

"Another time."

"Well, how about if we skip this floor and go up to the attic? We'll be very quiet — okay?"

Philip considered this, glancing down the hall to the closed door of the room where Helen lay in bed. "All right, then. But no more tapping, please."

# 13

Miranda threw open all the windows to let in the fresh breeze. "Mmm," she sighed. "It always smells so good after a storm."

Dan roamed around the attic. "Lot of junk up here, but I bet some of it's museum material." He trailed his hand along the low bookcases under the windows. "Did you bring these old books and stuff with you? Look at this mechanical bank!"

Miranda walked to his side. "They were here when we moved in." She leaned on the bookcase and felt Dan watching her as she gazed at the treetops blowing in the breeze outside. She had felt Nicole's presence in the attic as an intrusion, but she wanted Dan here. Maybe she and the dollhouse had been alone for too long. Having Dan beside her seemed to ease the close atmosphere of the attic. Having Buddy along helped, too . . . But where was he?

Miranda went to the head of the stairs and peered down. "Buddy? I thought you came up with us." There on the bottom step sat Buddy. She hurried down to him. "Hey, Buddy. What is it?"

"I'm not going up there." His voice was defiant.

"Why not?"

"You'll laugh," he predicted sulkily and turned his face to the wall.

She touched his shoulder and sat next to him on the step. "I promise I won't."

"Well, *he'll* laugh, then." He cast a glance over his shoulder up the stairs.

"No, he won't. I won't let him."

"I'm scared." He met her eyes, and she saw it was true.

"Of the attic?"

He nodded.

"Why?"

He hesitated. "I—I don't know. There's like something—waiting. I have this weird feeling." They sat quietly for a minute, then he smiled at her. "Hey, you really didn't laugh."

She shivered. "No." A thought struck her. "Will you come up with me, Buddy? I'll stay right with you. I just want to show you something."

"What?"

"The old dollhouse your aunt was talking about. The one the slave made before he moved on."

"I don't care anything about old dollhouses!"

"I just want you to look at it, and . . . tell me what you think."

He mulled this over, staring apprehensively up the

stairs. Dan appeared in the doorway at the top. "Having a cozy chat?"

Buddy stood up abruptly. "I had to get a drink of water," he said with dignity.

They climbed the stairs. Miranda led the way to the dollhouse corner. "There," she said. "What do you think of it?"

Dan knelt in front of it. "Mandy! This is amazing! It's really old—a museum piece, for sure." He looked up at her. "It's the dollhouse the carpenter slave made, isn't it?"

She nodded.

"Why didn't you say anything when Aunt El first mentioned it?"

Miranda just shrugged.

"Is it really a copy of your house?" asked Buddy.

"It really is," she told him. "But not exactly the way our house is now—it was built almost a hundred and fifty years ago. Our house has a bigger porch. And the dollhouse doesn't have the same kitchen, either, because the one in our house was renovated in the 1940s—and the downstairs bathroom was added on."

"My parents would give anything to have this for the museum, I bet," said Dan. "How much would you want for it?"

"It's not for sale." She looked at it with new appreciation and recalled the story of the slave who had made it. His gift had been one of love and thanks—why should the house now hold so much terror?

"She needs it to play with," said Buddy. "Right, Mandy?"

"Um — right," she said.

"Oh, yeah?" drawled Dan. "You seem too old for dolls, but it does look like you're all set up for some heavy-duty play, with the fan and those cushions. Is that what you're doing over here all the time? Playing?" His voice was teasing. He peered behind the house. "But where are the dolls?"

A feeling of panic swept over her. Forget about merging raindrops. She had to get them out of the attic. "Let's go down now," she said.

Buddy edged toward the stairs.

Dan looked at her oddly. "How can you play house without any dolls?"

He would never be able to understand. But Buddy sensed something. Maybe Buddy would see what she saw. "Buddy," she called, "wait a sec. Come back and look at the house."

"I saw it."

"Come see it again."

"I don't like dollhouses," he stated flatly.

"Just for a second."

He returned reluctantly. Miranda nudged Dan aside and positioned Buddy behind the house. "Now, you stand here," she instructed. "I'm going to stand on the other side of the house — and you look through the windows here and tell me if you see me."

"Why?"

"Just for fun," she returned, blushing under Dan's amazed stare.

"Now that's what I call fun," said Dan.

"Please, Buddy. Then we'll go downstairs."

145

She ignored Dan's incredulous face and positioned herself in front of the house. Buddy stooped down to peer through the dollhouse attic windows. She saw his face at the little windows and waved to him. He waved back. Dan waved at her, too. What an idiot he must think her!

Buddy came around from behind the house. "Okay? Can we go now?"

Miranda nodded, her face flame-red.

"Well, that was really fun," said Dan. "Wish we could play that game more often."

Miranda jammed her fists into the pockets of her shorts and didn't answer.

"It's lunchtime," Buddy announced. "Let's go, Dan. I'm hungry." He headed toward the stairs.

"Bye," she said, and slumped down onto the cushions behind the house. Footsteps hurried down the stairs and, far away, Miranda heard a screen door slam. Dan probably thought she was insane and would never come back. And that was fine with her, despite the moment in her cellar when she thought she might end up liking him better than any of the boys she'd known in New York.

She had the dollhouse—she didn't need any more than that.

"Tell me about it." The voice startled her.

She jerked her head up. "I thought you went home!"

Dan sank to the floor next to her. "May I have a cushion?" he asked politely.

Wordlessly, she handed him one.

"I saw Buddy out," he said. "Since the hostess forgot her manners."

Miranda stared at the floor. "I know. I'm totally rude."

"Yeah."

She looked up at him. "So why bother to come back?"

"Because I like mysteries."

"What?"

"You are such a mystery!"

She almost smiled. "You mean, I'm such a weirdo."

"Right." His eyes met hers. "Friendly one minute, weird the next."

"What do you mean?"

"Oh, come on. Look at it from my angle for a minute. Here we get new neighbors in the old Galworthy house at last. When we get back from vacation, we invite them over. And one of them is a great-looking girl my age. But she's totally unsociable, really gives me the royal brush-off. She stays inside all the time. I think: Maybe it's my hair? And so I get it trimmed. I think: Maybe she doesn't like my shirt? I make my mom buy me a new shirt! I think: Maybe she just doesn't like boys, and maybe I should forget her, but I think, Go for it, Dan Hooton. At least go over and ask her out to a movie.

"So then today, when I'm wearing my new shirt and planning to come over to see you, you arrive at our door and finally seem to want to be friends! You even invite me over—okay, me and Buddy, but he more or less invited himself, right? I start thinking, good, maybe she really does like boys. Maybe she'll even come out to see a movie. But then you get all weird again. And do you know when you got weird? When we started talking about this dollhouse, is when." He ran out of breath and sat there, searching her face, his own expression serious.

Miranda laughed weakly. What was she supposed to say to all this? "So—you want to know if I'll go to a movie with you? What's playing?"

"Forget that for now," he said. "First of all, I want to know what's going on with you." He sounded determined to get what he wanted, and Miranda felt a flicker of panic.

She fought it down. "Listen," she told him. "You won't believe me in a million years. You'll think I'm totally insane."

"Yeah, a real lunatic. But I'm all ears."

She stood up and paced restlessly around the attic. What did she have to lose? So what if he thought she was crazy? She had been alone with the dollhouse for too long now. Its magic had stopped being an exciting secret and was becoming a burden. She still didn't know why she had this power to see the past, and she didn't have a clue about what she was supposed to *do* with the power. Just watch? Or something more? Maybe Dan would have some ideas.

*Don't tell!* the dollhouse seemed to shriek—but another voice, one in her own head, cried: *Yes!*

"Okay, then, listen. It all began when we moved here—at least part of it began then . . ."

Dan settled himself on the cushions. He watched Miranda move around the room, but he did not speak.

She told him the whole story, beginning with the very first night in the new house when she had peered through the dollhouse attic windows and seen the dressmaker's dummy. She told him about the Kramers and the Galworthys — all she knew of their lives from the scenes she saw. She explained how she could sit there behind the house for hours, watching.

"I asked Buddy to look through the windows because he's sensitive to the atmosphere, somehow," she concluded. "But he didn't see anything. He just felt frightened — and you'd better not laugh at him, because I've felt frightened, too. It's an unbelievable thing to be able to see the past through the dollhouse, and it makes me feel very lonely to know that it's only happening to me. That I'm all alone in this."

She sat back down on the floor near the dollhouse and fell silent.

Dan traced a floorboard with his finger. "It's impossible," he murmured.

"See? I knew you wouldn't believe me!"

"It sounds like science fiction. It's not that I think you're lying — at least, you have no reason to lie to me. But I think you must be mistaken, somehow. What you think you see isn't really there."

"Oh, I get it — I'm not lying, just hallucinating! You believe I believe I see what I see. Thanks a lot."

"You make it so complicated," he said.

"Listen, I see what I see because it's *there!*" She frowned at him. "Or was there. But I know I'm not

149

crazy." She wondered if maybe she were, if maybe feeling sane had nothing to do with whether you were crazy or not. But no, no. Aunt Belle had felt something in the house. And Nicole. And Buddy . . .

Dan touched her on the knee. "Mandy, I'd love to believe you. It's the whole business of time travel, you know. The subject fascinates me. But it's science fiction! I'd have to see something for myself to believe what you're saying."

"Then you don't believe in what you can't see?"

"Right."

"Then you don't believe in electricity—or sound waves, or molecules—or even God!"

He looked away. "It's not the same thing at all."

"It is exactly the same!"

Dan frowned and rubbed his temples. Then he sat back and looked at her. A slow smile spread across his face. "Okay, Mandy. How about this? We'll do an experiment to prove you really see into the past."

"But I've already done one." She explained how she had put the crumpled newspaper balls on the floor in front of the house and how when she looked through the windows from the other side, she'd seen Dorothy in the attic playroom. But when she'd put the balls in the dollhouse itself and looked in at them, she saw only the paper.

"Yeah, yeah," said Dan impatiently. "But that only proved things to *you*. My experiment will prove it to me, too."

Miranda listened to his plan. It seemed easy enough.

She was to look into the Galworthy house and describe to him exactly what she saw — paying special attention to furniture and household items.

"You see," Dan continued, "it seems to me that if you're really seeing into the Galworthys' house as it was in 1904, some of the things you describe will match pieces in our museum. I don't know much about the Galworthys, but I do know a lot about the museum. I know that before old Sigmund Galworthy locked up the house and left Garnet for good, he gave a lot of his family's belongings to my ancestors — the ones who let him stay in our house."

Miranda felt excited. "I get it! You'll check in the museum to see if any of the things I see are there. What a great idea!"

Dan smiled modestly. "Oh, it was nothing. Wait till you hear about some of my better ideas."

She relaxed next to him, feeling better about the whole mystery and about him, too. "Let's wait and see if it works, first, before I award you a Nobel Prize."

"We could win one for this. We really could!" he grinned. "Think of it — we'll have proved you can see what no one can possibly see — into another time!"

"When I asked about it at your house this morning, everyone seemed to agree that time travel is impossible."

"It's not actually time travel, though, is it?" mused Dan. "I mean, even if what you say is true, you don't actually *go* anywhere. It's more like — like museum exhibits! As if time were preserved in a case for you to look back on."

A shiver pounced up Miranda's back. "But why me?" she pressed.

Dan gave her a long, measured look. "Because you've got great legs?"

She threw a pillow at him.

# 14

Her parents' bedroom was dim when Miranda peeked in after lunch. Helen lay flat on her back, staring at the ceiling.

"How are you feeling?" asked Miranda.

"Better," Helen answered with a trace of the smile she used to have before moving to Garnet. "Sit down, Mandy." She patted the bed and pulled a pillow behind her head.

"What is it?"

Her mother answered with another question. "What were you doing up in the attic?"

"Talking to Dan Hooton. He just left."

"I'm glad you're getting to know the neighbors, honey — but why in the attic?"

"We were looking around for the secret room that Mrs. Wainwright says is here somewhere." She recounted the story of the airtight room and the fugitives who had almost died there.

Helen shut her eyes for a moment. "What a close call! Those poor people!" She rearranged the pillow under her head. "Listen, Mandy. It's fine with me if you and Dan want to explore the house. But I don't like the attic. I don't want you going up there."

"What do you mean?"

"I don't know." She adjusted the pillow again. "I just don't like this house anymore. It's a strange atmosphere — don't you feel it? A . . . waiting atmosphere. As if someone were waiting for something."

"Waiting for what?" cried Miranda. "Oh, Mither — "

"Waiting and brooding," said Helen slowly. "Poor Belle was right, I'm afraid."

"I don't think anyone is . . . waiting."

"Belle warned me that something was wrong with the house — she said we should leave. I got a letter from her yesterday. She said she has no other explanation for what happened to her here, but everything is back to normal since they left this place."

"Mither, you're scaring me!"

"I always have headaches here," continued Helen, as if she hadn't heard Miranda. "I never used to be sick at all in New York. Sometimes I feel so . . . strange here. Not like myself at all. I forget things. Little things like your tomato sandwich. For some reason I felt sure you didn't like tomatoes. And I get these angry flashes of wanting something I can't have, but then when I really think about it, I don't know what it is I want! I had a fight with Dad this morning while you were gone — I was furious he wouldn't let me have a job. Mandy, what I was saying was crazy! My work is why we moved to Garnet. I have a career I love! I wasn't making any sense at all." She fingered the sheet, pleating it. "These days I always feel like I'm going in and out of a fog."

Miranda froze. Lucinda. Iris. Her own mother? All having headaches. All disliking the house, wanting to leave. All, unbelievably, making some kind of fuss about tomatoes. And now this business about jobs . . .

She stretched out a hand and smoothed back her mother's hair. "Don't worry, Mither. Don't worry." She said it as much to comfort herself as to reassure her mother.

"Stay out of the attic, Mandy. Promise me."

Miranda hesitated. "I can't," she said gently. "I don't get headaches and I'm feeling fine. There's no reason for me to stay out of anywhere."

Helen sighed and sank even further into her pillow. "I suppose you're right. I'm letting my imagination get the better of me." She closed her eyes wearily. "I'm just so sorry we moved here."

Miranda stared at her for a moment, then left the room. She walked quickly up the attic stairs.

Miranda searched for the Galworthys but encountered Kramers instead in every room, in every season. After a few minutes of changing from room to room, she gave up trying to find the Galworthys and resigned herself to the Kramers' attic. Dan's experiment would have to wait.

Timmy and Jeff Kramer, dressed in pajamas and slippers, stood in the middle of the black-curtained attic, howling. Jeff ran to the door and pounded his fists on it. After a minute or two the crying subsided. Jeff stopped his pounding, and Timmy stopped kicking the floor. They sat together quietly.

"I hate her, I hate her, I hate her," Timmy whispered fiercely. He turned on his brother. "If you hadn't spilled her perfume, we wouldn't be here!"

Jeff began to cry. "I didn't spill it! She only *said* I took it, but I didn't!"

"Yeah, but then you went and said *I* must have spilled it! Liar! Liar! Jeff is a liar!" His voice rose in a hysterical singsong.

"You shut up!" cried Jeff, and he pounded on the door again. After a second, Timmy joined in, and the din grew thunderous. "Mommy, Mommy, Mommy!"

Just as Miranda noticed the sturdy new latch that had been installed on the door, the door flew open, sending both little boys sprawling. Iris Kramer, her hair wild, stormed in on a wave of magnolia perfume.

"I've had it with you, you little brats! Any more nonsense out of you and you'll stay up here all night!"

Miranda clenched her hands into fists. She had seen this before, heard this before, even *smelled* this before.

Timmy and Jeff began to cry again as Iris towered over them, her hand raised to strike.

"Don't hurt me, Mommy!" screamed Timmy.

A doorbell, very faint, chimed downstairs. Iris paused. "Any more noise out of you two and you'll really answer for it," she said coldly and walked to the door.

Far away, the door chimes sounded again. The attic door closed; Miranda heard the scrape of the new latch. She felt sick.

"I'm scared," whimpered Jeff.

Timmy sat up. "Don't cry, Jeff. Don't cry. Daddy has just gone to the town meeting. He'll come home soon and let us out."

"Mommy said Daddy will spank us!"

"You know he won't. Mommy just said that because she has a headache."

"She always has a headache," said Jeff. "She didn't used to."

"She doesn't like it here. She wants to move and get a job."

"Mommies don't have jobs! They have to stay home with their children."

"Well, she wants a job. I heard her tell Daddy the house gives her a headache. If she had a job she wouldn't have to be home."

"I don't like it here, either!" Jeff peered around him. "Timmy! It's dark in here!"

"Shh! It's all right."

"It's dark, it's dark!" Jeff's cries took on a note of panic as his fear of the dark closed in on him. He ran to the door and had raised his fists to hammer again, when Timmy caught his arms.

"No," he said softly. "Do you want *her* to come up again?"

Jeff lowered his arms and burst into fresh sobs. Timmy searched his pockets. "Look, don't cry. Look!"

He held up a box of matches. "Light! I found these on Daddy's desk. We can make a torch."

Jeff brightened. "We can make a fire?"

"We could light up some of those old papers—roll them up, you know, into a big stick to carry around."

"Yeah, okay!"

They set to work gathering the yellowed newspapers and twisting them into tight rolls. "Just like Daddy makes to light the fire in the fireplace," observed Jeff, perking up.

Timmy considered this. "You know, we could probably build a fireplace out of those old suitcases in the corner."

Miranda refrained from closing her eyes, not wanting to lose the scene. She feared for the little boys' safety—feared she was about to witness the fire that blackened the attic so long ago. If only she had some way to warn the boys of the danger!

Timmy and Jeff soon had a small blaze going in the corner. They fed it with bits of newspaper. "There," said Jeff, satisfied with their work.

"Now it isn't dark," added Timmy after a while.

A tongue of flame lapped around Timmy's slipper, and Miranda sucked in her breath. Those stupid kids! "Watch out!" she shouted, forgetting they couldn't hear her. Timmy moved his foot and stamped out the small flame. He fed another twist of paper to the fire.

"You know, the fireplace downstairs has a chimney," he said to Jeff, looking rather concerned about the smoke that now swirled around them. "Maybe we should try to make one, too?"

But Jeff wasn't listening. "Hey, come here!" he called, waving his brother over to the wall. "Look at this little crack in the floor!"

Timmy went to look, all concern about chimneys forgotten. Just then the tall flames leapt out of the corner and crackled along the dry wood of the floor. The boys jumped back as the flames traveled across one wall and caught a box of old clothes. "Watch out!" screamed Jeff, as sparks flew out around them.

The smoke grew dense as the clothes smoldered and burned. "Water!" screeched Timmy, choking.

Jeff ran to the windows and pulled back the black curtains. He tugged at the locks. "Help! Help! Let us out!"

Just as the smoke became so dense that Miranda didn't see how the boys could have lived to return to Boston, the attic door crashed open, the latch torn from the wood. Iris and Andrew Kramer rushed in, gasping and shouting through the smoke.

"Timmy! Jeff? Where are you? Quick!" Crying and coughing, the boys ran toward the sound of their parents' voices. Jeff fell before he reached the attic door and was snatched up by Iris.

"Oh, my baby, my baby," she moaned, running down the stairs with his limp form in her arms.

Miranda collapsed back onto her cushions and turned the fan on high. She coughed wrackingly and stumbled over to the windows. So that was what happened! Because Iris locked her children up in the dark attic, they'd almost died. Had she ever forgiven herself? Miranda fervently hoped not.

# 15

Helen went to her office the next day still complaining of a headache but determined not to delay the opening of her new practice. Philip and Miranda sat together in the sunny kitchen, Philip with his nose in the paper, Miranda eating breakfast. Miranda shook some more cereal out of the box and splashed a generous amount of milk over it. "What are you doing today, Dad?"

He looked at her over the newspaper. "Oh, this and that. Anything I feel like. You know—the happy life of the unemployed."

"Yeah, you sure sound happy about it." Miranda's tone was ironic.

He groaned and laid the paper on the table. "I don't know, Mandy. I love puttering around, but maybe I was wrong to give up teaching."

"Don't tell me you're ready to go back!"

"No, not really. I haven't been happy teaching for the past few years. But it feels very strange to be home while Mither goes to work."

"She makes enough money. You could stay home and take care of the house."

"I guess I'm more old-fashioned than I thought," he replied. "I certainly don't mind if she makes more money than I do—any doctor makes more than a teacher. But I just don't see myself staying home, either."

Miranda liked having her father confide in her this way, though she wondered whether he would be this open with her if her mother weren't being so remote and unfriendly. He probably didn't have anyone he could talk to anymore.

"Why not give yourself the summer to think about what you want to do?" she said. "Wasn't that your plan, anyway?"

"You're right." He pushed back his chair and smiled at her. "Sensible Mandy, that's just what I'll do. There are at least a dozen odd jobs needing to be done outside and around the house. Just look at those overgrown hedges!" He swung his arm toward the windows.

The day outside glistened. Water droplets from yesterday's downpour gleamed like tinsel on the long blades of grass and hedges in the side yard. Miranda spooned the last morsels of cereal out of her bowl and carried the dishes to the sink. A tap on the window-pane above the sink startled her, and she glanced up. Dan waved cheerfully, then appeared at the open screen door.

"You're early," said Miranda. "Come on in."

"I had to sneak away while Buddy was still eating

breakfast," he explained, then greeted Philip and sat down at the table.

"I like Buddy!"

"You've only seen his company manners."

Philip stood up. "Well, I'm off to attack the wayward shrubberies."

"Oh, wait—Mr. Browne?" Dan shifted his chair and looked up at him. "I almost forgot! Dad said to ask if you'd be interested in going with him to Lexington today, if you're not busy. Somebody has donated a collection of Revolutionary War era clothing and books to the museum, and my dad has to sort through everything. Since you used to teach American history, he thought maybe you could help him decide what's valuable and what's not."

Philip's face lit up. "That sounds a lot more interesting than cutting the hedges down to size. I'll go give him a call." He hurried out of the room.

Miranda held out a stoneware bowl full of fruit. "Good timing. Dad was just saying how bored he was getting with being a house husband!"

Dan selected a peach. "Well, after breakfast Mom and Buddy are going to town to do errands and go out to lunch, and I figured with your dad and mine in Lexington and your mom at work, we'd have some privacy for trying the experiment. Not to mention finding that secret room."

"Come on upstairs," she told him. "Speaking of the experiment, I have a lot to tell you."

They carried their peaches up the stairs. "Did you do it?" he asked.

"Not exactly. But I've found out some interesting stuff." Miranda switched on the fan behind the dollhouse and arranged the cushions on the floor.

Dan settled back, adjusting a pillow behind his head. He bit into his peach. "Ah, this is the life," he grinned. "Let the entertainment begin!"

Miranda recounted what she had seen in the Kramers' attic the evening before. Dan listened carefully without interrupting. She was describing the fire and smoke when she stopped abruptly in midword and stared at him openmouthed.

"What is it?"

"Oh, Dan! I just remembered something!" She jumped up from the floor. "What a complete idiot I am!"

"What is it?" he repeated excitedly.

She turned to him, glowing. "I know where the secret hiding place is!"

"You do? *How?*"

Miranda crossed the attic to the blackened walls on the far side. "Timmy and Jeff built the fire here because they were afraid of the dark—it was practically pitch black in here that night with the black curtains, and the switch for the lights is out on the landing. Jeff called for Timmy to come look at something—a crack in the floor . . ."

"A trapdoor? Is that what you're thinking?"

"Yes!"

"Why didn't you look last night?" He began walking along the wall, examining the floor.

"Just when he said that, the flames flared up and

caught some clothes on fire — and the smoke got so bad I couldn't think about anything else."

Dan sniffed. "It doesn't smell like smoke now."

"Of course not. The fire happened about fifty years ago!"

He shook his head. "Oh, yeah."

Miranda scanned the blackened floorboards. "The fire wasn't really bad — it was the smoke that was dangerous. I mean, the Kramers didn't have to move out because of the fire. It's not as if the whole house burned down."

"Well," mused Dan, "if it happened the way you say it did, then probably Iris Kramer felt too guilty to stay here."

"I hope so," said Miranda staunchly. "She deserved to feel guilty. She seemed so nice when they first moved in, but then she started to change . . ."

Dan was inspecting the blackened floorboards. "No trapdoor here."

Miranda dropped to her hands and knees. "No — it was over here. Let's see. They built the fire in the corner — and then Jeff walked over here . . ." She crawled along the wall. ". . . To here. Where this camping stuff is." Miranda bent down to push the sleeping bags and boxes of equipment out of the way, and Dan helped. Together they slid it a few feet across the floor.

"Got bricks in these backpacks, or what?" asked Dan.

"Could be. Mither saves everything." She pushed aside an enormous new cobweb stretched between a box and the wall and wiped her dusty hands on her shorts. "Spiders are fast workers," she said. She pointed: "There!"

Dan examined the long crack. "I think you've found it, Mandy! This is it!" He traced his finger around the edge. "It's hardly noticeable. And there's no ring or handle or anything to pull the door up with, just this little depression in the wood for a finger-hold."

"We need a lever," said Miranda, hugging herself. "I think Dad's still here. I'll go see if he has something in the toolbox."

She returned minutes later with Philip behind her. He looked intrigued and brandished a crowbar. "Your dad and I are leaving in a half hour," he said to Dan. "But let's see what you two have found here." He knelt on the floor and peered at the crack. "Well, what do you know!"

Miranda and Dan stepped back to give Philip more room. He levered the crowbar into the widest part of the crack and wiggled the tool back and forth gently, careful not to splinter the charred floorboards. "Okay," he said finally. Miranda and Dan knelt next to him, placing their fingers in the widened crack.

"When I say, *now*," said Philip, "pull up as hard as you can."

They braced themselves firmly on their knees and waited. Philip positioned the iron bar. "Okay, one, two, three . . . *now!*" He jerked down the crowbar and at the same time Miranda and Dan lifted with all their combined strength, but the floorboards did not move.

They sat back, perplexed. Then Dan bent over the crack once again. "Wait a sec! Let me try something!"

He pressed down firmly on the floorboards. They heard a *click*. He grinned and sat back. "Okay, now try it!"

Miranda stuck her fingers in the crack and pulled. The heavy square of floorboard inched open.

"You did it!" cried Miranda.

"A hidden locking mechanism," explained Dan, glowing with satisfaction. "There's a sliding panel in our museum wing that opens just.like that when you press on it!"

"Good thinking!" Philip helped Miranda raise the trapdoor on its old hinges, and they propped it open with a suitcase.

A dark hole greeted them, and a rush of foul air made them wrinkle their noses. Miranda leaned eagerly over the edge. "Look, it's like a little tunnel!"

In the morning light streaming through the attic windows they could make out a narrow passageway only a few feet long, leading into a tiny room under the eaves. "Wow," breathed Dan. "And I thought the secret room in our house was tiny! This is just a *hole*."

"You wouldn't want to hide there for very long," agreed Philip. "You can tell it's airtight just by the way the door fits."

"I'm going down," said Miranda.

"Wait a minute, Mandy," Philip cautioned. "We don't know yet how safe the floorboards are. I don't want you crashing through."

"Come on, Dad," begged Miranda. "I'm lighter than either of you. And I found it first!"

"Okay, okay! Just hold on while I get a flashlight. It'll be too dark to see anything at all without a light."

When he had gone, Miranda and Dan turned to each other expectantly. "Isn't it great?" Miranda grinned.

"You are brilliant, Sherlock."

"Thank you, my dear Watson."

Philip clattered back up the stairs with a large flashlight. "I'm afraid the batteries are low."

"Oh, it doesn't matter!" cried Miranda, nearly snatching the flashlight from him. "I'm going down now!"

She stepped cautiously into the hole. "It seems strong enough," she said. "I'll have to crawl through the passageway to the little room. No way can anyone stand up in here."

"Careful, Mandy," warned Philip. "Test the boards first with your hands before putting your full weight on them."

Miranda dropped to her knees and moved slowly along, feeling her way. What air there was in the tiny hole was fetid with a strange odor she could not identify. "Ugh," she complained. "It really is foul in here."

"It's been shut up for a long time," said her father. "It's probably not a good idea to breathe it in."

"Well, what should I do? Hold my breath?"

"Just take it slow."

Miranda slid out of sight.

"Hey," called Dan after a moment. "What's it like?"

"Dark!" she called back. "Wait a sec—these batteries really *are* low." Her voice sounded muffled. "And it stinks, and—oh!" she broke off. "There's something in here! A pile of old clothes—"

She shone the dim light onto the heap in one corner of the tiny chamber and caught her breath in a ragged gasp.

Illuminated in the circle of light lay a small, huddled figure wrapped almost entirely in a tattered gray blanket. One tiny hand was flung outside the blanket—and long blonde curls fanned out across the floor. Miranda dragged her eyes away, and a low moan of horror filtered back to her father and Dan. She recognized that hair; she had seen those long blonde curls before. A wave of nausea surged around her as she fought her way back along the narrow passageway, striking her head on the low ceiling. She emerged into the waiting arms of her father and Dan, who lifted her out onto the attic floor.

"What is it, Mandy? For God's sake, Mandy!" cried Philip. He gathered her against him, as Dan wordlessly lowered himself into the hole.

Miranda sat quiet, then after a moment struggled to get up. Tears streaked her face and she was shockingly pale. She shook her head. She couldn't speak.

Dan returned, scrambling through the hole, two bright red spots of color livid on his cheeks. Philip clutched his shoulders, half lifting him out.

"What's wrong, Dan? What is it?"

Dan collapsed on the floor next to Miranda and closed his eyes to blot out the nightmare. "It's a dead girl," he said faintly.

# 16

When the police arrived they surged upstairs, measured the hidden chamber, and removed the body. Downstairs, two calm officers interviewed Miranda, Dan, and Philip, and then they talked with Ed Hooton, who had raced across to the Brownes' house at the first appearance of police cars. The trip to Lexington was off.

The chief of the Garnet police force sat in the living room and asked Miranda and Dan to relate how they had discovered the secret room. Another officer sat at the chief's side taking everything down in a scratchy shorthand. They were excited. Nothing much of interest happened in Garnet—a bicycle theft or two was all the police department usually had to investigate. And here was—well, not murder, perhaps, but a mystery. It was exciting news on a sleepy Garnet summer day. A third police officer telephoned the newspapers in Garnet and the surrounding towns. Even the Boston reporters would want to be in on this; it would put Garnet on the map.

Miranda and Dan explained how they found the room, leaving out the part the dollhouse and the Kramer family played in leading Miranda to the trapdoor. Philip offered the further information that the Brownes had been living in Garnet for the past four weeks, just moved there from New York.

"Who was she?" wondered Philip. "And how did she come to be in that room?"

"That's just what we aim to find out," said the police chief, a woman around Helen's age, with sharp green eyes and short black hair. "We'll contact the man who sold you the house. Name of Kramer, I believe. We'll keep in touch with you, of course. Let you know what we come up with. And I'll have someone stop by your wife's office and tell her the news. Your daughter looks like she could use both her parents just now."

"That's okay," muttered Miranda. "I'm all right."

The chief stood up and shook hands with Philip. "I'm sorry this had to happen in your new home," she said as she left with the other officers. "Not a very nice housewarming."

Mr. Hooton slung his arm around Dan's shoulders. "Do you two want to come over to our house?" he asked. "Though I suppose the reporters will be over there in a flash if they don't find you here."

"I think we'd better stay here until Helen comes home," Philip answered. "Why not stay with us for now? I'll get us something to drink."

Helen arrived to a front porch swamped with reporters clamoring to be allowed upstairs to photograph the hole.

She pushed past the throng of cameras and ran into the house, locking the door. "Phil? Mandy? What's going on? Is anybody hurt? The police stopped by my office. They said there was a dead body!"

Philip put his arms around her and explained. Miranda watched as her mother's face grew pale. Helen shook her head. "No, no! That's too horrible to be true."

Miranda and Dan and their fathers led her up to the attic and showed her the trapdoor. Helen absolutely refused to go down. But Ed Hooton slipped into the tunnel with the flashlight to see the tiny room and the chalk line the police had drawn around the body before removing it. Philip's weak attempt at a joke fell flat. "Last year I would have been too fat to get into that tunnel. Now I'll fit—but I find I don't want to."

Downstairs again, Helen was still pale but her voice was strong. "I knew it," she insisted. "What did I tell you about the attic? I knew there was something wrong! Something was waiting up there all the time."

Ed Hooton looked at her in surprise but said nothing. Philip put his arms around her shoulders in a brief hug. Miranda felt Dan's eyes on her, but she didn't look at him.

Hours later the reporters and photographers departed, finally satisfied that the Brownes and Hootons had nothing to tell. The lane grew quiet again. Miranda walked Dan and his father back to their house across the road. As Ed Hooton climbed the steps to their porch, Dan turned to Miranda. His eyes were dark with distress. "We didn't bargain on that, did we?"

She stepped nearer to him and tentatively touched his arm. "That hair—"

"I'm just glad I didn't see the face. Did you see it?"

"No. Thank God. But you could tell she was young."

Suddenly Dan had his arms around her in a fleeting hug. Then he stepped back. "See you tomorrow?"

She nodded. "Yes."

She watched him run up the steps, then she walked slowly back home. Helen was stirring soup in a pot on the stove; Philip sat at the table.

"Well," he said, rubbing a hand over his face, "you were right, Helen. I'll never say another word against women's intuition as long as I live."

"I *knew* something was up there," she affirmed. "Waiting and biding its time."

"Oh, Mither! You're giving me the creeps!" cried Miranda.

Her father reached up and stroked Miranda's hair as she stood beside him.

"You've had a bad shock today, Mandy. I think an early bedtime is in order."

"I'll never be able to sleep," she muttered.

"There's nothing to be gained by staying awake and thinking about it," he said. "Look at it this way. That child's body was here for a long time, and we never knew it till today. But now it's gone—there's no sense starting to feel uneasy about it *now*."

Helen set a bowl of fragrant vegetable soup in front of him. "Oh, right, Phil!" she said sarcastically. "I know I, for one, won't be giving that long-dead

172

mummified body a second thought." She put her hands on her hips. "Come on! How can we help thinking about it?"

The telephone rang then, and Philip went to answer it. "Hello?" He listened for a second. "Yes, Chief Patterson."

Miranda and Helen strained to overhear.

"Yes, yes. I see." Philip's voice was soft. "Well, that certainly changes things, doesn't it? Yes, yes indeed. Please keep in touch. We'll want to know how things develop."

"Well?" asked Miranda as soon as her father had hung up. "What did she say? Did she talk to the Kramers? What did the Kramers say?"

"Whoa! Slow down." Philip took his seat at the table again. "Chief Patterson called Timothy Kramer, who lives in Boston with his wife and children. He and his brother are the ones who inherited this house last year when their father died, and they put it up for sale. Mr. Kramer lived here for a year when he was very little—four or five. He couldn't remember much about it, actually. He said they never knew anything about a trapdoor or a secret room. His parents moved the family back to Boston shortly after there was a fire in the attic."

Miranda's thoughts raced on ahead. Little Timmy Kramer was all grown up and living in Boston with a wife—and children! He would be older than her own father. And he said he knew nothing about the trapdoor—and yet he and his brother were the ones who'd led her to find it. Could it be he really didn't remember?

Philip ate his soup while he talked. "One thing the chief did say, which pretty well rules out any connection with the Kramers, anyway, is that the coroner has looked at the body and determined that the child was seven or eight years old when she died, and they think she died around the turn of the century!"

"Goodness!" exclaimed Helen. "That long ago! I wonder what could have happened, poor thing."

Miranda ate her soup in a daze. It couldn't be true — it *couldn't* be! And yet she'd felt the sick shock of recognition when her flashlight illuminated that golden hair. There was no mistaking it. Records showed that Dorothy and Lucinda Galworthy had been killed in the train wreck. But somehow, incredibly, little Dorothy had died in the secret hiding place under the attic floor.

Miranda feared she would lie awake all night reliving the horror of the day's discovery, but as soon as she got into bed, she was asleep. Toward morning she fell into a dream — a haunting dream of twisting corridors through which she wandered, searching for her mother. It seemed Helen was always just ahead out of sight, and Miranda ran faster to catch up to her.

"Mither!" she called again and again, but the figure ahead did not hear and did not stop. "Mither!" she called, but her voice came out a harsh whisper, hardly loud enough to be heard.

Finally the corridor ended and the figure in front of Miranda was forced to stop. At last, thought Miranda. She tried to run even faster, but her legs seemed to gel, and she moved in slow motion, as if under water. At the end of the hallway was a single bright spot, a small window through which the yellow sun shone. Helen stopped in front of it and turned to face Miranda. She held out her arms and Miranda ran to them, anxious to be within their comforting circle. The arms tightened around her and she felt momentarily secure. "Oh, Mither," she cried. "I tried so hard to get back to you!"

She raised her face to look at her mother. Helen smiled gently and tightened her grip. Slowly, as Miranda watched, Helen's smile widened until it no longer resembled a smile at all but was a grimace, teeth bared. The arms holding Miranda grew painfully tight, and she struggled to get away. She tried to scream, but no sound came from her throat. Laughter filled the air... Helen was laughing, her strength squeezing the breath out of Miranda.

With a moan, Miranda jerked back and forth, trying to escape. She awoke, panting in the morning light. Her body was drenched in sweat.

The room seemed strangely still. After a moment she could hear her alarm clock ticking, and from downstairs came the morning sounds of her parents making breakfast. A blender whirred, a cupboard door slammed. Miranda hugged her pillow.

A short time later the front screen door banged.

Miranda forced herself to get out of bed. She looked out the window. Helen was walking down the porch steps on her way to work. Just as she reached her car in the driveway, she turned and looked up at the house, catching sight of Miranda's face in the window. She raised her hand in a wave, which Miranda automatically returned. Then Helen slid into the driver's seat and swept her car smoothly out into the road. Miranda slumped onto the window seat.

What an awful dream! As if in a trance, she walked into the bathroom and shed her nightgown. She stepped into the shower to wash off the traces of sweat and fear. Afterward, feeling considerably more normal, she dressed and went down to the kitchen.

Philip sat sipping his diet milk shake and reading the newspaper at the kitchen table.

"Morning, Mandy." He smiled. "Did you sleep all right?"

"No," she told him. "I had nightmares."

"I don't wonder," he comforted her. "I think none of us slept very well." He handed her the *Garnet Star*. "But look at this. We've made the front page!"

MUMMIFIED CHILD FOUND IN GARNET ATTIC
Mystery surrounds the discovery of a mummified child that lay hidden in a secret attic room of a Garnet Township home for nearly a century.

Yesterday afternoon police removed the remains of a small girl from the old Galworthy House, now home of Mr. Philip and Dr. Helen Browne and their daughter, Miranda. Miranda, 13, and a neighbor, Daniel Hooton, 14, discovered the body in a secret room beneath the attic floor.

In a statement to Police Chief Margaret Patterson, Mr. Browne said he had "absolutely no idea who the child could have been." Police are still researching the history of the Brownes' house in hopes of finding a clue leading to the identification of the dead girl.

Anyone with any information is asked to contact Chief Patterson at the Garnet Police Department.

A second front-page article gave a brief history of their house and mentioned that the Brownes had only recently moved to Garnet from New York City. But Miranda only skimmed it. "Anyone with any information — " She lowered the newspaper and felt her father's eyes studying her.

"I'm going out for a ride, Dad," she said. "Maybe up to the old graveyard."

"I don't know, Mandy. Why not ride into town? You can go shopping for some school clothes — get your mind off yesterday." He reached for his wallet. "Here, let me give you money for a new skirt or something."

"Thanks, Dad. I'd love a new skirt, but not now." She kissed him and headed for the back door, not failing to note the worry clouding his eyes. She knew he wished yesterday had never happened — wished he had the power to make everything all right for her now as he had been able to do when she was little.

"*Don't* worry, Dad! I promise I'll be back by lunchtime," she said.

She pumped her bike up the hill toward the open countryside. She sailed past miles of fields of young corn and finally wheeled onto a dirt road. The old Garnet cemetery lay to her right, nestled between the fields.

Miranda braked and laid her bike down on the grass. The cemetery was bordered by a crumbling wall, with leafy ferns like green waterfalls cascading over the rough stone. She gazed at the marble monuments inside, straight rows of white and gray stones and grassy mounds leading back from the graveled drive all the way to the fields of corn. Beyond them stretched the endless woods. The stones where she stood looked new, shiny, and straight. She wandered farther back among the graves. The older ones all seemed to be in a corner near the field. She assumed that the blackened sandstone and granite indicated age. The oldest markers were thinner than the others, and they leaned at various angles. She made her way among the crooked stones and thought that, far from being a scary place, the graveyard was quite peaceful. Under the bright summer sun it seemed possible that the spirits here could rest.

She meandered up and down rows, noticing the familiar names. A great number of Hootons and Wainwrights were buried here. She stopped once to look at the stone of a young Daniel Hooton who had died in the Civil War. She wondered whether he had helped his family hide the runaway slaves in their secret room under the stairs. By the time she had circled back to the more recent graves, she was thinking about the modern-day Daniel Hooton. She wished she'd asked him to come with her today.

Still, she hadn't found what she was looking for. She returned to the older corner beyond the modern stones for a more thorough search and finally came to what she knew must be here: a section of the cemetery full of Galworthy stones — some old, some more recent. She read each one as she passed: "Julian Galworthy, Our Blessed Babe. d. 1810, Aged 5 months." "Anne Elizabeth Galworthy, a Good Woman. d. 1870, Aged 67 yrs." "Myron Galworthy, Who Died With Rosy Cheeks in the Seventh Year of His Age, 1866."

"It's got to be here," she muttered to herself, examining each stone carefully. Then she shook her head. "But it *can't* be here. It doesn't make any sense."

She stopped suddenly at a sleek gray stone and drew a sharp breath.

In Memory of

SIGMUND GALWORTHY

born in Garnet 1869

died in Boston 1942

Poor Sigmund. He had never recovered from Dorothy's and Lucinda's deaths. Miranda moved on to the next stone — and gasped, sinking to her knees in front of it. Here it was. She traced each letter lightly with her finger.

In Loving Memory
LUCINDA WALKER GALWORTHY
Nov 1873–Jan 1904
and
DOROTHY ARABELLA GALWORTHY
July 1896–Jan 1904
Beloved Wife and Daughter of Sigmund Galworthy
"THE LORD GIVETH AND THE LORD TAKETH AWAY"

"But the Lord didn't take Dorothy away!" Miranda exclaimed aloud. "At least not *then!* Poor Dorothy didn't die in the train wreck with Lucinda—she *couldn't* have! Or else how could she have died in the attic?"

"A very good question," said a low voice at her side. Miranda screamed, leaping up from the grass as if a whole army of ghosts had materialized before her.

"Take it easy," drawled Dan. "I was only agreeing with you!"

She clutched him with relief and buried her face on his shoulder. "God, Dan! That's the second time you've snuck up on me!"

He wrapped his arms around her. "Hey, anything for a hug!"

She pulled away and dropped onto the grass in front of the gravestone. "I was just wishing I'd asked you to come with me! And here you are."

"Your wish is my command." He sat cross-legged next to her and picked a long spear of grass.

"How did you know where I was?"

"I called your house, and your dad said you'd come up here." He stuck the blade of grass in his mouth and spoke around it. "He's worried you're being morbid."

"Do you think I am?"

"We have good reason to be." He examined the gravestone. "Mandy! Don't tell me these are the people from the dollhouse!"

"They are. But, Dan — " She told him about recognizing Dorothy's hair and about Chief Patterson's phone call. "See? I knew it was Dorothy when I saw her — but what the chief says proves it. That girl died at the turn of the century. The calendar in the Galworthys' kitchen said January 1904!"

Dan traced the dates on the stone. "That's when she was killed in the train wreck, right?"

"But we know she didn't really die in the wreck!" Miranda stared at Dan, her thoughts tumbling to be expressed. "Oh, God, do you think *that's* why the dollhouse is magic — ? I mean, do you think Dorothy has been haunting the dollhouse because she was trying to tell me she was in the hidden room and wanted to be buried properly?"

Dan lay back and flung an arm over his eyes. "What was she doing in that little room, anyway? I can't believe any of this."

"You've got to believe it! I know, Dan — let's try to ask her."

"*Ask* Dorothy? What are you talking about?" He sat up and glared at Miranda.

"Don't look at me like this is all my fault," she

scowled back at him. "It's just an idea."

"You mean sit here in the graveyard and have a séance?"

"Sort of! We'll just try to reach her and ask her how she came to be in that hiding place and what we can do to help her now." She smiled encouragingly. "Come on. How can it hurt?"

He groaned. "I'm beginning to see why you were a social recluse. You were trying to protect your poor neighbors from total weirdness!"

"Listen, nothing was ever weird in my life until the day I moved to Garnet," she retorted. "You've lived here forever, so you've got to help me!"

"I don't follow the logic on that one," he said. "But okay. What do we do first? Light a candle? Find a crystal ball?"

"We hold hands." She had never done anything like this before. Was it even possible to contact spirits? Were there really such things?

"Hey, great!" He grabbed her hands.

"Come on, be serious."

"Right. Sorry. What next?"

"Well—we close our eyes and think about her. You just be quiet now, and let me do the talking."

"Be my guest!" But he held her hands firmly and closed his eyes. Miranda closed hers, too, and sat for a long moment. Somehow, as they sat there, she could feel the teasing draining right out of Dan. She knew he *was* trying now, trying to reach Dorothy. She pictured little Dorothy in her old-fashioned dress, with her long blonde curls tumbling over her shoulders, playing with her ball.

"Dorothy?" she whispered.

But then the image of the withered little body she'd found the day before intruded. She opened her eyes to find Dan looking at her.

"I keep seeing the body," he whispered.

"Me, too," she murmured. "But let's try again."

She closed her eyes, gripped Dan's hands, and drew a deep breath. "Dorothy? Dorothy?" Her voice was louder now. "We want to help you, Dorothy. We know you didn't die in that train wreck. We found you in that awful little room. Can you tell us what we should do now? Shall we have you buried properly here with your mother and father?"

The wind picked up and whispered through the stalks of corn in the fields. The birds sitting on the stone wall took flight, chirping as they flew overhead. Did Miranda imagine it, or was the still, summer air suddenly cooler, alive with—something? She felt Dan try to pull his hands away, but she held his fingers tightly.

"Dorothy? Tell us what to do." But it was hard to picture Dorothy, and hard to concentrate with all the sounds stirring up the old graveyard.

A squirrel chattered at them from the top of a stone in a nearby row. Two bees buzzed past, their hum loud in Miranda's ear. Dan pulled back and opened his eyes, and Miranda opened hers. The whole cemetery seemed alive with the buzzing and humming of insects, the chatter of the squirrels, the chirps of the birds. The wind blew harder, rustling the long grass around the stones.

"She didn't answer," said Dan loudly above the sudden cacophony. "See? End of experiment!" He jumped to his feet.

Miranda stood up and wiped her hands on the seat of her shorts. She walked silently next to Dan, back to their bikes by the stone wall. She couldn't stop gazing all around her at the scolding squirrels, at the birds hopping from stone to stone.

"Sounds like the whole place has come to life!" said Dan, mounting his bike. "I bet we're in for some more rain."

Miranda rode down the hill with the wind in her face, her ponytail flying behind like a long ribbon, her mind in a tangle. She had almost grasped something there in the graveyard, something that slipped away. "End of experiment," Dan had said. But was it? Or had Dorothy answered after all?

# 17

The notes Miranda played that afternoon at her flute lesson were not crisp and clear, but blurred and faltering. The lilting piece she was to have learned by heart came out sounding choppy, off-key, with the end forgotten entirely. Miranda found herself blinking back tears. Mrs. Wainwright stopped her and placed a wrinkled hand on Miranda's shoulder. "I don't blame you, my dear," she said. "There's been a lot of excitement up at your house—and not very pleasant excitement, from what I hear. You shouldn't expect yourself to be in top form after such a shock."

At the gentle touch, Miranda's tears flowed, and she put down her flute and sobbed openly. Mrs. Wainwright had her arms around Miranda in a second, patting her on the back. "There, there, let it out now."

"It was awful! I didn't even see the face, but the hair—I just keep seeing it in my mind!"

Mrs. Wainwright sat with her until she stopped crying. "I—I'm sorry," Miranda said finally. "I didn't practice very much this past week, and I meant to work really hard yesterday. But then we found—it. And I forgot all about playing."

"I understand perfectly," said Mrs. Wainwright, her old face creased in sympathy. "Let's just forget about it for now. But I'm hoping to have you ready to play in the autumn concert—you know, that's Garnet's big fund-raiser for the library. So how about if you work on your piece all weekend, and we'll see at our next lesson how you're doing. I want you to be note perfect by this time next week, my dear!"

"I will be," Miranda assured her, feeling much better. Then she said good-bye and left the house. She pedaled down the street as fast as she could, then up the hill toward home.

No one had been in the attic since the day before. Miranda hesitated at the top of the stairs, breathing in the hot, foul air that had been released from the tiny chamber. Two fans whirred on high speed; they had been left on all night to air out the attic room. But as far as Miranda could tell, the smell was as strong and as sickening as ever. She tried to push the memory of yesterday's discovery out of her mind. Her throat felt dry.

The atmosphere in the attic had changed. Miranda could now sense the *waiting* that had so repelled her mother. And yet, rather than sending Miranda running away, the dollhouse seemed to be beckoning to her. Once she was behind the dollhouse, in another time, she knew the awful smell would disappear. She would try to find Dorothy, try somehow to ask her how they could help. She settled herself on the cushions and looked through the kitchen windows, hoping for the sugary-spice smell of Hannah's oatmeal cookies.

But what she saw was Iris Kramer chopping onions at the kitchen table. Usually Iris wore soft cotton print dresses with cap sleeves and demure collars, but now she was wearing a dark blue skirt and suit jacket. The jacket fit snugly over her white tailored blouse, and the whole effect was that of a uniform. She chopped the onions into a pile, then reached for a heavy black frying pan crackling on the stove and slid the pile into the hot fat. Andrew stepped into the room, scowling. Timmy and Jeff pushed in behind him.

"Iris?"

"What?" She placed the pan back on the stove and turned to him. "Oh, you brought the boys home?"

"Obviously. I saw them in the front yard playing with the Hooton kids, and they told me Timmy and Jeff couldn't go home until you were home. I asked where you were and was told you'd left the boys with Betty Hooton while you went out to work!" He eyed her suit. "What's going on?"

"Well, I was just about to go over and get the boys myself. I came home only a few minutes ago and wanted to get supper on the stove." She pulled out a chair for him at the table. "Andrew, honey, sit down." The boys grabbed apples from the centerpiece bowl and ran out of the room. "I've been meaning to tell you, dear. I've got a job."

"Iris! Without telling me?"

"I only started just the other day. And it's only three days a week." Her voice tightened. "I should think you'd want me to be happy."

"Iris, of course I want you to be happy. But what is this job? Where do you work?"

"It's right in town. At the bank. I'm a secretary!"

Andrew sat back in his chair and adjusted his glasses. "A secretary! Iris, I didn't know you could type or take shorthand, or that you had any interest at all in office work. We don't need the money, dear. I would really rather you stayed home with the boys."

She glared at him. "Well, I'll have you know I can type very well! And we can always use more money. With this war, who knows when even you might be called up, and then I'd be here without any means of support."

"It's hardly likely I'll be called, Iris. You know how bad my eyesight is." He sighed. "Listen, why the secrecy? What's happening with you?"

She lowered her eyes. Her voice was very soft. "I can't stand it, any of it. This house . . . the boys . . . I have to get out."

"This doesn't sound like you!" he exclaimed. "You've always told me how delighted you are with our life, with our children. You always used to go on about what a little homebody you are! Honestly, Iris, I some-times wonder —" he broke off at the sight of her face.

Her eyes were narrowed in fury. Red blotches of color stained her cheeks. She slammed the pan of on-ions down on the table, narrowly missing Andrew's hand. She hissed at him, "You try to stifle me—to hold me down—but I won't let you. You can't keep me here! I am not your chattel! I *will* work, Andrew Kramer, and you just try to stop me!"

Miranda moved back from the dollhouse and leaned against the wall. She felt bone-tired. She rubbed her scalp. Even her hair, she thought, felt tired. This wasn't helping Dorothy at all. Miranda wished she knew what Dorothy wanted from her.

She went downstairs and sat outside on the porch swing. As she rocked, she stared into the darkness of the bushes and listened to the tree frogs. They sounded louder than usual. She remembered the insects and birds and squirrels at the cemetery that morning—remembered, too, her feeling as they left. Maybe Dorothy had given her a message after all. But what could it be?

She had tried to reach Dorothy, tried to ask what she wanted. She had suggested they find a way to have Dorothy buried with her parents. It was then, just then, that all the rustling and buzzing and chirping and humming started. Could Dorothy have caused that to happen?

She looked at her watch. It wasn't too late, really; she would call Dan. Funny how she'd come to rely on him in the past few days. She went inside to the kitchen phone, pausing to stare at the stovetop where, only moments before—or so it seemed to her—Iris Kramer had been stirring onions.

"Can you come over for a few minutes?" she asked Dan. "I need to talk to you. I've been thinking about the cemetery."

"Uh-oh," said Dan. "Sounds like a very *grave* situation."

"Just get over here!" Nothing was funny anymore. She hung up.

On her way back out to the porch to wait, Miranda was stopped by the sounds of quarreling. She closed the screen door gently and sidled back into the front hall. Her parents' voices rang out from behind the closed door of the living room.

Philip sounded exasperated. "Helen, what the hell is wrong with you? *I'm* the one who is currently unemployed, not you! If anyone is going to sit around whining about wanting a fulfilling career, it should be me! You're not making any sense—you don't sound like yourself at all!"

Helen's voice, when it came, was so low and biting that Miranda doubted for a moment that it was her mother in there. "I know what you're trying to do, Phil! You're trying to keep me under your thumb! You think you own me! You try to stifle me—to hold me down—but I won't let you. You can't keep me here! I am not your chattel!"

Miranda backed away, her heart knocking in her chest. Talk about repeat performances! She raced out onto the porch, straight into Dan.

# 18

"We've got to do something!" she cried. "Something's really wrong with my mother!"

They stepped back inside the house. Miranda listened. Only silence. "What's happened?" asked Dan.

"Sshh!" she said. "Let's go up to the attic."

They climbed the stairs quickly. Dan hesitated at the top but then followed Miranda over to the dollhouse. He kept his eyes averted from the hidden room.

Once they were seated on the cushions behind the house, Miranda covered her face with her hands. "Dan, I'm getting scared."

"Tell me what's going on! You said you wanted to tell me something about the graveyard?"

"That's why I called you to come over in the first place—but it doesn't seem important now. What's important is my mother—she's not acting like herself."

"How do you mean?"

Miranda shivered. She drew her knees up and wrapped her arms around them. "Dan, this is getting way too weird. I mean, it's strange enough that I can see things through the dollhouse, but when the same things I see start happening in my own family—! What am I supposed to do?"

"Is your mom acting like someone in the doll-house?"

"Mither just about repeated word for word what I heard Iris Kramer saying tonight! And Iris was going on about the same thing Lucinda Galworthy did, years and years before that!"

Dan knelt to peer into the dollhouse. "You sat here and watched, and then you went downstairs and heard your mom say the same thing Iris said."

"Right. Iris was yelling at Andrew about how she wanted a job—anything to get out of the house. And that's what I heard Mither going on to my dad about."

Dan opened one of the little bedroom windows, then slid it carefully shut again. "Did it ever occur to you that maybe it's just a coincidence? Maybe Iris wanted a job. And maybe your mom wants a job. That's not so unusual."

"Dan!" She grabbed his arm. "Will you listen to me? She *has* a job. She's an obstetrician! She has her own practice—that's why we moved to Garnet in the first place. Sometimes I think her job is her whole life. She works all sorts of weird hours and is always rush-ing off to deliver babies in the middle of the night. I could understand her yelling about *not* wanting to work anymore. But she was yelling at my dad that she wants to get a job!"

He studied her. "You're right," he said finally. "That's totally bizarre. Do you think she has forgotten somehow? I mean, like does she have amnesia?"

"I don't think so. I think something is making her say these things. *Compelling* her to."

"And do you have any idea what?"

Miranda shrugged, but the tingling had started in her stomach, and she thought she could smell Lucinda's magnolia perfume. She stood up. "I do have an idea. Let's try to contact Dorothy again — and this time we'll ask her what's happening with Mither."

"You mean go back to the graveyard?"

"No. Dorothy's not there, anyway. We should do it right here." She pointed to the trapdoor. "Over there, actually."

"How? There's no way I'm going down that hole, Mandy!"

"Please, Dan?" She heard the strain in her voice. "We won't go inside. We'll just sit near the entrance. Please?"

"The things I do for you."

They sat against the wall by the windows, about six feet from the hole. It wasn't hard to keep their eyes shut; neither one wanted to see the gaping black space. Nor was it hard to keep a grip on each other's hands; neither of them wanted to pull away and sit alone.

Miranda tried to picture Dorothy — to conjure up those blonde curls without summoning the nightmare image of the body they'd found. Dorothy had been a little girl. She had lived in this house, had played up here. Her father loved her, and she loved him. Her mother seemed too angry about all the injustices she perceived in her own life to pay any attention to what was happening in her daughter's. And somehow Dorothy had died in that little room. Had she been playing? Or hiding? Why had no one found her? Only a little girl. And she had died too soon.

"Dorothy?" Miranda whispered.

They waited. Miranda was holding her breath. She let it out slowly and tightened her fingers on Dan's. "Dorothy, are you here? Can you help us? Do you know what is happening to Mither?"

Dan stirred. When he spoke, his voice squeaked. "Dorothy?" He cleared his throat. "We'd like to know how we can help you, too. We don't understand what happened to you—and we don't understand what's happening to Mandy's mom. If you know, please tell us!"

Miranda half expected the attic to come alive with the sounds of insects and birds, the way the graveyard had that morning. But the room was still. No breeze wafted through the open windows. No cars drove by on the street. There was no sound at all.

But then there was a smell. Miranda sniffed. She opened her eyes, her heart thumping madly as she recognized what it was.

Magnolia.

She pulled her hands away from Dan's and jumped up. The panicky feeling of being chased assailed her, and she bolted for the stairs. "Run!" she screamed, and they clattered down together.

Philip and Helen were standing in the hallway.

"Mandy!" Philip grabbed her as she flew past him. "What were you doing up there?"

She skidded to a stop and leaned against him. "Oh, Dad!"

"You weren't down in that awful hole, were you?" Helen's voice echoed the panic Miranda had felt in the attic.

"No, Mither! Of course not." She took a deep, calming breath. "We just wanted to — to see it."

Dan stepped forward. "It's just so hard to believe it really happened," he said, as if by way of explanation.

Did he mean hard to believe they'd found the body? Or hard to believe they smelled that magnolia? Miranda glanced at the attic door. Her heart hammered under her thin T-shirt, but the scent of magnolia was gone.

Helen closed the door firmly. "It's late," she said. "Time for you to be going home, Dan. And Mandy? I want you two to stay out of the attic from now on. It's no place to play."

"No problem!" said Dan. He said good night, and then Miranda accompanied him downstairs to the front door.

"No place to play," she murmured.

"You can say that again," he said.

"But it was Dorothy's playroom!"

"And look what happened to her! It's a creepy

place." He went out onto the porch. "At least your Mither seems all right now, even though the experiment didn't work."

"But you did smell it, didn't you?" She had to be sure.

"Smell what?" He looked at her closely. "You smelled something? Is that why you ran?"

She looked out at the trees in front of the house and nodded.

What could he say? He had smelled nothing. He had run out of the attic only because her panic was contagious. He hugged her now, briefly, and turned to go. She imagined she could see relief like a ribbon of light streaming behind him as he raced away from the old Galworthy house, back to the haven of his own.

# 19

Miranda didn't sleep well that night. She felt hot and kicked off her sheet. Then the wind picked up and blew through the window, chilling her bare legs. She dragged the sheet back up and pulled the bedspread over her as well. After she was asleep the wind dropped again, and the air in the room grew close and stuffy. She woke up, kicked the covers off, and tried to find a cool spot on the bed. She tossed around miserably until morning, not exactly dreaming, but thinking about Dorothy each time she awoke and wondering whether she should tell the police she knew who the dead girl was. When morning came and she awoke again, she was all wound up in the sheet. She untangled her legs and sat up, rubbing her eyes. She felt bruised.

Miranda looked out the window and saw that the car was gone. That meant Helen had already left for her office. She peeked into her parents' room to see if Philip was still asleep, but the bedding was tossed around as if he and Helen, too, had had a sleepless night. The room was empty.

Good—no one to be disturbed by her music. She set her flute case on her desk, opened it, and lifted out the instrument. If anything could make her forget about Dorothy and Lucinda and all the weirdness, it was Vivaldi.

She pulled her music stand out of the corner and set it up in front of the window, then opened her sheet music to the piece she was to learn for the concert. She moistened her lips, held up the flute, and began. At first she was distracted by the sight of Dan's house through the trees across the street, but soon the piece began to work its magic. She no longer looked out at the world, but inward, to the music.

She didn't know whether what happened when she played was a strange thing or not—maybe, indeed, all people experienced the same sort of thing when they concentrated on something important to them. But when Miranda played her flute, she would find herself falling into the music, into the story it told. After the first few minutes of warming up, she no longer noticed her fingers on the keys or her mouth on the mouthpiece, controlling the flow of air. Instead, she was off in some other place, listening to the music as if she herself were not playing it, but as if it flowed through her from some other source. Hours of practicing could pass this way, and she would return from this other place only when something jarred her—a wrong note or an outside disturbance.

What stopped her this time was an outside disturbance: a light patter of applause behind her.

She stopped playing, blinked, and lowered the flute. "Dad! I didn't know you were there!"

Philip laughed. "I took care that you didn't. It isn't every morning that I'm treated to a concert."

"I'm practicing·to play in the autumn concert—a real concert, Dad. To benefit the library."

"Well, you're in fine form. That was just beautiful."

"Thanks!" She gathered her sheets of music.

"Don't let me stop you, Mandy. I just came up to say it's lunchtime, and I'm leaving now with Ed Hooton for Lexington. We're going to try again to check out some stuff that's been donated to the museum. He thinks I'll be helpful as an advisor."

"I'm quitting now, anyway. My mouth is all dry." She licked her lips.

"We'll probably be back in time for dinner. Mither called and said she'd like you to put the roast in the oven around five o'clock so it will be ready when she gets home. I've left it thawing on the counter by the sink."

"No problem, Dad."

"Set the oven to three hundred and fifty." He kissed the top of her head. "See you later!"

She put her flute away and went down to the kitchen to make a sandwich. As she sat eating it, she felt the lure of the dollhouse upstairs pulling at her, stronger than ever. *Come up, come up,* it seemed to urge. And, carrying her sandwich, she obeyed.

Miranda settled herself on the cushions and peered into the kitchen. She was immediately enveloped in the aroma of freshly baked bread. Two fragrant loaves lay on top of the black cast-iron stove in the Galworthys' kitchen. The oven door was closed, but the warmth of the kitchen told Miranda that more bread was baking inside. The windows in the kitchen were steamed halfway up each pane; the scene outside was white. Snowflakes drifted across the glass. The calendar on the far wall read "January 1904" and had a picture of people in bright winter scarves riding in a sleigh pulled by a team of spirited horses.

Miranda looked into the living room, searching for the Galworthys. A bedraggled Christmas tree leaned in one corner, its ornaments drooping. Boxes half full of candles and other tree decorations lay strewn on the floor, and Miranda guessed that Hannah had left her clean-up job half done. She waited, looking through the living-room windows for a few minutes, but Hannah did not return. Miranda moved on.

In the master bedroom upstairs she caught her breath sharply. The scent of magnolia was overpowering. She braced herself to keep the panic at bay. "I will *not* run away, I will *not* run away," she chanted in a whisper.

Lucinda sat before double mirrors on a small lacquered stool, brushing out her waist-long auburn hair. She hummed softly to herself. After several more slow strokes of the brush, she shook her hair back and gazed appraisingly at her reflection in the long mirrors.

"Mirror, mirror, on the wall," whispered Miranda.

But Lucinda could not have looked less wicked. She smiled happily at her reflection, then dipped her tapered fingers into one of the array of glossy pots on the table and smoothed the curves of her delicately arched brows.

She fluffed back her hair and reached for a crystal vial. She removed the stopper. The magnolia scent intensified as Lucinda applied several drops of the perfume to her wrists, the hollow of her neck, and behind her ears.

Entranced, Miranda stared, almost forgetting her fear of this woman. "I wish I looked like that!" she murmured, regretting her own dark hair and suntanned face.

"Mama? Can I come with you?"

Dorothy stood in the doorway of her mother's room, wearing only a petticoat, her golden hair hanging in curls around her small face. Miranda stifled a gasp of horror. That golden hair . . .

"Your grammar, Dorothy," answered Lucinda, not turning away from the mirrors. "You'll never get ahead in life if you don't speak properly."

"*May* I come with you? Please?"

Lucinda's smile disappeared as she spun on the stool to face her daughter. "No, you may not, Dorothy. Why aren't you dressed? I want you ready to go on time, do you understand? I'm taking you over in half an hour."

"But I want to come with you!"

"I said no. I am going away on a little trip—and you are to stay with Mrs. Hooton."

"No!"

"Dorothy, don't be difficult. With Hannah gone there's nothing else I can do but leave you with Mrs. Hooton."

"But what kind of trip? Where are you going?"

Lucinda hesitated, then caught her reflection in the glass and smiled. "Just a little business trip, my dear. It's time to make something of myself."

"When will you come home, Mama?"

Lucinda hesitated, then glanced again at her reflection in the mirror. "Soon enough," she said. "But if I'm not back before your father gets home, I'm sure he'll think to look for you at the Hootons'. I'll leave him a note. Now, hurry!" Before turning back to the vanity, she removed her robe and dressed in a gown of deep violet with black lace at her throat and wrists.

Dorothy wandered over to the vanity table and perched at her mother's side. "Please, Mama. I want to go with you! I'll be ever so good, I promise!"

"Don't wheedle!" snapped Lucinda. "Go get dressed immediately."

Dorothy sulked, fingering some of the little bottles on her mother's table. "I can't do up the buttons on my dress."

"Then get Hannah to do it—oh, bother!" Lucinda frowned in vexation.

"Hannah quit, Mama."

"I know that, you tiresome child!" Her voice became icy. "Get your dress and bring it here. I will do up the buttons myself."

Dorothy did not budge, but inspected the crystal vial of perfume, unstopping it and holding it to her nose. "Mmm," she said. She spilled a small amount into her palm.

Lucinda leaped from the stool and grabbed Dorothy's shoulder. Dorothy cried out and tried to twist away, tipping the bottle and spilling the strong scent over herself and her mother. Lucinda knocked it out of her hand with a snarl. "*Now* look what you've done, you hateful brat! You ruin everything you touch!"

Dorothy backed away toward the door. Lucinda grasped her wrist and pulled her over to the vanity table. "You will learn to obey me if it's the last thing I ever teach you." And with those words, she turned the child over her knees and lifted the frothy white petticoat. She grabbed the long wooden hairbrush from the vanity and beat Dorothy until the little girl's screams filled the room. Then she threw down the brush and yanked Dorothy out the door. "Up to the attic with you, my girl. I can see you're not fit to go visiting today."

Her voice and Dorothy's cries of "Don't hurt me, Mama!" dwindled as they vanished down the hallway to the attic stairs.

Miranda waited at the bedroom window, biting her lip in anger. Lucinda and her hairbrush brought back other memories—of Aunt Belle and the porch swing slat, of Iris Kramer and the wooden spoon. *It's as if*

*Lucinda were somehow ... contagious,* thought Miranda. *Was it Lucinda who infected them all? Was it really possible that someone could reach from the past to cause unhappiness for those who lived in the present? Or was it the house itself that was evil—the house that infected Lucinda as well as Iris and Aunt Belle and—?* Here Miranda stopped. She couldn't bear to think about her own mother.

Lucinda stalked back into the bedroom and sat down, picking up her hairbrush. She began twisting and piling her rich hair onto her head, securing the thick mass with countless hairpins. "Where are you when I need you, Hannah?" she muttered, as half the elaborate coiffure tumbled down around her shoulders again.

After checking and rechecking her appearance in the double mirrors, Lucinda left the room. In the hallway Miranda heard her call up to the attic: "I want you quiet up there, young lady. An afternoon in the cold will teach you to mind your mother!"

As Lucinda's footsteps descended the stairs, Miranda pictured little Dorothy locked in the unheated attic in nothing but her petticoat. She shivered, tears gathering in her eyes.

Rinky-dink piano music, sounding tinny to Miranda's ears, drifted through the house. Miranda moved along from room to room, peering out the dollhouse windows until she located Lucinda in the living room, seated at the piano. The time sequence had never remained chronological for so long before, and Miranda hardly dared to blink, afraid of losing the continuity. Lucinda was still wearing the violet dress.

"Monster," muttered Miranda.

Lucinda left the piano and went into the kitchen. Miranda found her there when she moved to the doll-house kitchen window. Lucinda checked the baking bread, then crossed to the wall telephone and lifted the receiver. She wound up the crank on the side of the wooden box and tapped a few times on the lever. "Operator? Operator, get me Garnet two-one, please. Yes, I'm waiting."

Lucinda's long fingers tapped on the tabletop. "Yes, yes. Hello, Mrs. Hooton. This is Lucinda Galworthy. I'm calling to say I won't be sending Dorothy over to you after all. But thank you so much for your kind offer of hospitality. It's very neighborly of you." Her voice was pleasantly cordial.

"I've decided to take Dorothy along with me," continued Lucinda. "She has always enjoyed train rides." There was a pause, then Lucinda answered gaily, "Oh, we're just traveling to Boston to visit my dear old auntie." After a few more pleasant remarks Lucinda replaced the receiver, smirking. "Dear old auntie indeed," she murmured, a smile tugging at the corners of her beautiful mouth. "Dear old auntie! Wait till I tell Donald." She left the room and the piano music jangled again. This time it was a dance tune.

Miranda was just turning away from the kitchen window to check on Dorothy in the attic, when a face appeared at the back door and the chimes sounded, clear and melodic. Lucinda entered the room again and hurried to the door. Miranda's head reeled when a man dressed in a gray overcoat came in brushing off snow, crying, "Lucinda, beloved!" as he pulled her into an embrace.

She held him at arm's length. "You're wet, Donald. And cold."

This scene! This was the first time the dollhouse had shown a repeat. As before, Lucinda left the room, returning a moment later wrapped in fur. Then the smell of burning filled the kitchen, and she snatched up a towel. "Oh, the bread! I forgot—!" She cursed sharply. "Damnation!"

Smoke whirled out of the stove as Lucinda shrugged to remove her coat, dropping it onto a chair. Then, there it was, the tiny *pinging* noise Miranda remembered from the first time she had watched this kitchen scene. Lucinda drew out the charred loaves and dumped them into the sink by the pump. "Ruined," she complained crossly to the stove, as if it, rather than she, were at fault. "You black monster!"

Donald was at her side, checking his watch. "My dear, calm yourself. It doesn't matter."

"Of all the rotten luck. I'll *never* learn to cook! Stupid Hannah! Why did she have to quit today of all days?"

Miranda raised her brows. "You awful woman," she shouted. "I'd leave, too, if I had to be around you for five minutes! You're wicked to the core."

But Donald was chuckling. "Darling Lucinda. A housewife you aren't! But where we're going, you won't need to be—" He embraced her, their cheeks touching.

Lucinda's voice sounded gay again. "Let's leave, then. We don't want to miss the train."

Donald helped her button up the fur coat. "But what about the kid? Where's Dorothy?" he asked. "She doesn't suspect anything?"

Lucinda's laughing features froze for an instant. "Oh—oh, she's over at the Hootons' and doesn't suspect a thing. Sigmund will bring her home. They'll be fine together. He dotes on her. They'll never miss me, I assure you."

Lucinda opened the back door, and a gale of wind blew snow onto the floor. "Just leave it!" she cried. "I'm never going to worry about keeping house again!"

"It'll be just you and me, my darling," Donald promised, ushering her outside. "We'll be in business together before you know it."

As they bustled out the door, Miranda heard the tinkle of Lucinda's laugh. "Oh, Donald, you'll love this! I told Mrs. Hooton I was going to visit my dear old auntie!"

Their peals of laughter were cut off abruptly as the door clicked shut.

# 20

Miranda sat back on her heels and rubbed her forehead. Then without a backward look, she ran downstairs, out the door, and across the street to the Hootons'.

Dan was in his room, stretched out on his bed, listening to his tapes. "Well, hello!" he greeted her, pulling off the headset. "Have a seat."

Miranda sat on the edge of his bed. "Oh, Dan. I've been watching again. It's all so awful—Lucinda makes me feel sick. Really, truly sick." She rubbed her forehead. "I tried to pay attention to the stuff in the rooms so we can check it out in the museum, but I couldn't concentrate. It's so terrible watching and not being able to do anything!"

Dan stared out the window at the gables of Miranda's house poking above the trees. "Listen, I'm really not up for any more séances—or whatever you call them. So I hope you're not here to suggest we try to contact Dorothy again. And, you know? I don't need to do my experiment to check in the museum. I believe you. How else would you have known where to look for that trapdoor, if you hadn't seen those Kramer kids point it out?" He paused, then confided in a low voice: "I had a nightmare last night."

"I haven't been sleeping very well, either," she admitted.

He touched the back of her hand. "So what did you see this time?"

She started speaking all in a rush, relating the scenes she had just witnessed in the Galworthy house—the way Lucinda had beaten Dorothy for spilling the perfume, how she'd locked the child up in the cold attic, how she'd waited for Donald down in the kitchen. "And then they left to catch their train—with poor Dorothy locked in that cold attic. I couldn't believe it! She just left her there!"

"That Lucinda sounds like *she* should have been locked up—for child abuse," Dan said grimly.

"I wonder if anybody knew how she treated Dorothy? She sounded like the sweetest thing on earth when she phoned Mrs. Hooton—your great-grandmother, right? In public she was totally friendly and polite. Nobody would ever suspect she was so horrible at home."

"Well, fortunately she had a maid to take care of Dorothy, so she wasn't actually with her that much alone, right? Sounds like old Lucinda wasn't the maternal type."

"She sure wanted a career." Miranda stopped. "I don't know—oh, Dan, it just makes me want to cry to think about Dorothy."

Dan shrugged. "But there's nothing we can do except to have her buried properly."

"How *did* she end up in that hole?" Miranda's eyes grew wide. "Do you think Lucinda murdered her?"

"Probably," Dan said darkly. "And if she did, I'd say the father and the maid and even my great-grandmother were to blame, too. They all should have noticed something was wrong in that house. They should have called the police — or the child welfare agency, or something!"

"Maybe they didn't have agencies like that back then."

"Maybe not — but they did have police! Anybody could have noticed that Lucinda wasn't exactly the perfect mother."

"But probably there's no such thing as the perfect mother."

"Are you defending Lucinda?" asked Dan. "I thought you hated her!"

"I'm not defending her! I was just thinking that maybe everybody saw she wasn't the greatest, but didn't think she was, you know, a *criminal*. That's all."

"Well, I don't buy it. People have a responsibility to watch out for kids and report something that looks suspicious. I bet Lucinda was abusive in lots of other ways, too — ways the dollhouse hasn't shown you."

"We don't really know for sure that Lucinda *did* kill Dorothy, remember." Miranda wasn't sure why she was protecting Lucinda. But the thought of a mother losing control—becoming a criminal—frightened her. Better to believe there had been some unimaginable accident. No one's fault.

She got up and paced around Dan's room. There were two shelves of books above his desk. One held several dozen science fiction paperbacks; the other held library books on the restoration and refinishing of antique furniture. She looked out the window and saw cars pulling up in the Hootons' driveway.

"You have company," she said.

"Patrons, you mean," he corrected, coming to stand beside her. "Want to join the tour?"

"Sure." Anything to get her mind off Dorothy.

Dan led the way downstairs, along a narrow hallway running the length of the house. "This connects the rest of the house to the museum wing. It was added in the 1890s."

Miranda glanced around at the closed doors and hallways leading off the one they walked down. "This house is huge!"

"Yeah, tell me about it. We have to keep a lot of it closed off in the winter because it's too expensive to heat." He stopped in front of a large oak door at the end of the corridor. "Here we are." He pushed the door open and they stepped into a bright foyer.

Mrs. Hooton stood next to a grandfather clock along one wall, speaking to a small group of people. Dan drew Miranda into the room, and Mrs. Hooton smiled a welcome at them before continuing. Miranda listened as Mrs. Hooton gave a concise history of the house, which was the prelude to the museum tour.

"After the Civil War ended and the Underground Railroad was no longer used to hide escaping slaves, the secret hiding places became favorite playrooms for children." Mrs. Hooton smiled at the visitors. "Generations of Hooton children have played in the secret room in our basement. My own boys used it until the museum opened and we turned it into an exhibit. We will go down in a moment." Her smile faded. "Of course, not all the hiding places in Garnet homes are as large as the one I'll show you today. Some were mere cubbyholes — airtight crevices where a slave could hide only a few hours."

Miranda's hand crept to her face. "Dan!" she breathed. "Let's go. I just thought of something."

He glanced at her curiously. "Okay." He flapped his hand at his mother and started around the group toward the stairway.

"Dan? Don't you two want to stay for the tour?"

"It's okay. I'll tell Mandy all the facts. I know the speech by heart!"

The visitors chuckled, and Mrs. Hooton joined in. One of the men detached himself from his wife and pointed at Dan. "Daniel Hooton? Didn't I just read your name in the newspaper? Aren't you the boy who found a mummy the other day?"

Interested faces turned to them. Dan nodded and took Miranda's hand. They left the foyer quickly, feeling the eyes of the crowd on their backs. Miranda was glad no one knew her.

Mrs. Hooton cleared her throat. "Yes," she said. "An

old Underground Railroad stop had some new excitement recently."

Miranda and Dan entered a low-ceilinged room hung with hand-stitched samplers and patchwork quilts. Along the walls, glass-sided cases displayed memorabilia of Garnet's past. Dan closed the wooden door behind them, cutting off the murmur of voices that floated up the stairs. He faced Miranda. "I always thought I wanted to be famous," he said. "But not like this. I don't want to talk to anyone about the... mummy."

"I was just thinking I'm lucky no one knows me around here," said Miranda. "They'll recognize your name and stop you on the street, but not me."

"I promise I'll introduce you," said Dan. "Maybe I'll make you a sign and pin it on your shirt: Ask Me About the Mummy's Curse. Something like that."

"Don't you dare!" Miranda sank onto a low cane-bottomed chair under the window, heedless of the Do Not Touch sign at the chair's foot. "Oh, Dan." Her voice was no longer teasing. "When your mom said how some of those secret spaces were airtight, it made me wonder whether Dorothy was only playing in the hiding place. Your mom said children liked to play in the secret rooms. Maybe she just got trapped down there. You saw how heavy that trapdoor is — maybe she couldn't get out again."

"You mean maybe Lucinda didn't kill her?" Dan shrugged. "Maybe. But wouldn't someone have come looking for Dorothy, in that case?" He scowled. "They'd call her for dinner or something. They'd come up and find her."

"But we know they didn't find her." Miranda stared out the window at her house across the street. The scene she had so recently witnessed through the doll-house windows nudged at the back of her mind. What was it about the Galworthys that day that struck her?

Suddenly it hit her. "Dan!" She jumped up from the chair and grabbed his arm. "Lucinda locked Dorothy in the attic and then left with that man—Donald—to catch a train. I heard him say they had to hurry so they wouldn't miss it. What if *that* were the train that crashed? Dorothy would have been locked in the attic, and no one would have come to let her out!"

"Her father would have come and let her out, though," argued Dan.

"No!" Miranda paced the room with excitement. "No, he never did. See, Lucinda and Donald ran off to-gether—and Lucinda was going to leave Dorothy with Mrs. Hooton until Sigmund came home from work. I heard her say that. But then after she went into her rage about that horrible perfume Dorothy spilled, and she beat her and locked her up in the attic, Lucinda called Mrs. Hooton and made up a lie that she was taking Dor-othy with her. But really, she just didn't want to tell her neighbor how she was punishing Dorothy."

"I get it," broke in Dan. "Then Lucinda was killed in the crash. If she hadn't died, then Sigmund would have gone home and searched for Dorothy. He would have heard her calling when he went into the house.

Even if she'd fallen into the hole, he'd have heard her and searched till he found her."

"But he didn't search at all, because Mrs. Hooton told him Dorothy went to Boston with Lucinda."

"And when he learned of the crash, he thought they'd both been killed . . ."

Their voices rose as they added to the story. But then Miranda shook her head. "There are so many things we don't know," she mourned. "Did Sigmund know Lucinda was going to leave him? Or did she tell him she was going to visit an aunt? If he didn't know anything, he would have been so shocked when the police came to his office to tell him of the train crash. He wouldn't have believed, at first, that her body could be in the wreck. But after he went to identify Lucinda's body, he would have rushed back to Garnet to get Dorothy. He'd assume Lucinda left her here with your great-grandmother. But when he got here, your great-grandmother had to tell him Dorothy went with Lucinda. It's so awful! Sigmund would have had to go back to try to find Dorothy's body, too."

"It's a tragedy," said Dan, "no matter how you look at it."

"The poor man," echoed Miranda, and fell silent. But then she stared at Dan. "But there are two bodies buried in the graveyard. We saw the stone! That means Sigmund somehow identified Lucinda *and* Dorothy! How did he do that—if Dorothy wasn't even on the train?"

"Oh, probably there was some other child who had

been very badly burned — maybe she even had blonde hair. Since Sigmund expected to find Dorothy, he did. I mean, he identified the burned child as Dorothy and had her buried with Lucinda."

Miranda nodded slowly, feeling swift compassion for the child interred under a name that was not her own. "I guess that's another of the things we'll never know," she said. "Mrs. Wainwright told me that since Sigmund couldn't bear to go home after he identified the bodies, he stayed here — with your great-grand-parents, I mean — for a few weeks."

"Weeks! And Dorothy was up in the attic the whole time — dying. No food. No water. She wouldn't have lasted long." He paled. "Makes you sick."

Miranda shivered in the warm room. "Poor, poor little girl," she whispered, wandering over to the glass cases along one wall and staring unseeingly through the top. "1896 to 1904, the gravestone said. Only eight years old. As old as Buddy. She shouldn't have died when she did. It wasn't time."

"I wonder if it's ever really time for anybody," Dan murmured to himself.

Gradually she became aware of what she was staring at. "Dan," she said slowly. He came quickly from the window where he had been gazing pensively at the old Galworthy house. "Look at this."

"What is it?" He peered over her shoulder into the case. "Oh, that old calendar."

"Not just any calendar! It's the one from the Gal-worthys' kitchen — January 1904!" She recognized the picture of the sleigh ride, the spirited horses, the field of snow.

"It could have come from any house," said Dan, pointing out the black-inked sign on the case which read: Local Household Items, Early 20th Century. The display included several pairs of wire spectacles, a heavy rusted iron, buttons and ribbons, a marble-handled letter opener, a teakettle, silverware, and a child's slate.

"It *is* the same one, though. Look what's written on it!"

Dan squinted at the faded, spidery writing. "January nineteenth," he read. "Sigmund to New York." He turned to Miranda, his voice full of wonder. "Wow, Mandy! This proves it one hundred percent." He looked at her with awed, almost frightened eyes. "Sigmund to New York. Maybe a business trip? I wonder if he ever made it."

Miranda turned away. "You already believed me; you know you did." She wandered around the little room. "God, it's just so unfair! Dorothy shouldn't have died then. It was just a series of accidents that killed her — despite Lucinda."

"Yeah, like a tragedy of errors," said Dan. "*If* she hadn't spilled the perfume, she would have been over at our house when the train crashed. Or *if* Lucinda hadn't lied to my great-grandmother about taking Dorothy on the train, or *if* Sigmund had gone home earlier and heard her crying in the attic — or hadn't stayed here for so long . . ."

"Or *if* Dorothy could have escaped somehow," mused Miranda. "Her death was such a mistake!"

"If you ask me," said Dan, "death is always a mistake."

Miranda stared at the calendar, thinking of Lucinda Galworthy, and wasn't so sure.

The voices of another tour group sounded outside the door, and Miranda and Dan exited another way, running down the back stairs and along a corridor to the lived-in section of the house. They climbed yet another stairway back to Dan's room.

"I'll give you the whole tour another time," he promised. "But at least we've accomplished something today. We know that my experiment worked, and we figured out what happened to Dorothy."

"You and your experiment," Miranda panted after all the running. "Dorothy is still dead."

"Come on, Mandy. She was dead for years and years before you and I were even born!"

"Well, she shouldn't have been!" cried Miranda.

"Don't yell at me! I didn't kill her!"

"I know, I know! I just feel I'm supposed to *do* something. You know, change things."

Miranda was looking at him but seeing instead the trees blowing in the cemetery the day before, when the wind picked up. She heard again the rustling and buzzing of insects, the frenzied chattering of the squirrels. "We wanted to fix things for Dorothy by burying her properly," she said slowly, a whole new concept forming in her mind. "We tried to contact her to ask what we could do to make her rest in peace. But what if that's not what she wanted at all? We just said it—Dorothy died too soon. It was a mistake. It shouldn't have happened. Dan, that's it!" She grabbed his arm and looked up into his face, her own eyes glowing with certainty. "She doesn't *want* to rest in peace. She wants not to have died in the first place!"

He looked at her intently. "Any plans, professor?"

Her face fell. She pleated the bedspread between her fingers in silence.

A breeze stirred the curtains. Then Dan leaned back on his elbows. "How long have your parents been married?"

She bunched the fabric in her fist, then smoothed it out again. "Oh, I don't know. About fifteen years, I guess. But why?"

"Well, it seems to me that if I went back in time about fifteen or sixteen years, to the time and place where your parents first met, and if I waited until just when your father was about to introduce himself to your mother, and then at that second I interrupted him and dragged her off to dance with me or something—well, they wouldn't have met!"

"Sort of like in that movie, *Back to the Future*?" Miranda laughed. "But my parents met on a bus, can you believe it? Sat next to each other. They were both really young—Mither was on her way to medical school, and Dad had finished college but didn't have a regular job yet. They ended up in New York and in love."

"The point is, if I'd sat next to your mom first, they wouldn't have met just then. And who knows? If they didn't meet each other then, maybe they'd never have met at all. Maybe they'd each have met someone else and married different people, instead of each other. Think of it! Then you would never have been born!"

"Thanks a lot," said Miranda glumly. "That would have been great."

"All I mean, Mandy, is that if you changed the past you'd be changing the present, too."

# 21

Catching sight of Dan's bedside clock, Miranda gasped at how late it had grown. "I'd better get home," she said, jumping up from her cross-legged position on Dan's bed. "I should have put the roast in the oven a half hour ago. Oh well, we can order out for pizza."

"Come over again tomorrow, okay? We can bike somewhere — but nowhere near the cemetery, okay?"

"Okay. I'll come over right after breakfast. I have to practice my flute in the afternoon, though, for the autumn concert."

"Famous Mandy." He reached for her. She squeezed his hand and headed for the stairs.

At the front door she turned to him, her forehead creased. "Listen. I've been wondering," she said. "Do you think we should tell the police that the body we found is Dorothy's, and that someone else is buried in the cemetery?"

Dan considered this for a moment, then shook his head. "We don't have any real proof. Nothing you saw through the windows would hold up in any kind of court—I can barely believe it myself. It just sounds like—"

"Total weirdness," finished Miranda. "I know."

"But it does seem wrong, somehow," Dan conceded. "Since we can't change what happened to her, the least we could do would be to bury her under her own name."

"But that isn't what Dorothy really wants," insisted Miranda. "I know it isn't. She isn't a ghost needing to be laid to rest or anything—she's a ghost who needs not to have died in the first place!"

"Well, you work on it," Dan teased. "Nothing you do would surprise me anymore!"

She ran across the lane, thinking about that. Could it be that she—and no one else—had the power to see into the past, for some reason? And what other reason could there be, except to rectify a wrong done decades ago? Yet what could she do to change the past? And—as Dan had mentioned—how might that affect the future?

Miranda was still deep in thought as she entered the kitchen. A wave of magnolia perfume immediately assaulted her, and a hard grip on her arm wrenched her out of her musings.

"There you are!" shouted Helen in a voice Miranda had never heard her use before. Helen's eyes glittered bright and wild, and her usually soft mouth was tightly drawn. The magnolia scent—Lucinda's scent—was overpowering. She shook Miranda roughly.

222

"Where have you been?"

Miranda tried to twist out of her mother's grasp. "I was over at the Hootons'!"

"At the Hootons'. I see. So considerate of you to leave me a note." Her voice crackled with sarcasm. "I had no idea where you were, young lady. You didn't even see fit to come home in time to put dinner in the oven."

"I'm sorry, Mither —"

"Sorry! I'll bet you're sorry! Off running around with some boy, leaving without permission, shirking your duties at home — that's sorry?"

"Stop it!" shouted Miranda. "I didn't do anything!"

"Didn't *do* anything!" mocked Helen, her eyes gleaming. "Didn't *do* anything! So, we add lying to the list, do we?"

"What are you talking about? I haven't done a thing! Honest!"

Helen fairly spat out the words. "Then I am to suppose it was a *ghost* who spilled my new bottle of perfume? And a *ghost* who neglected to put dinner in the oven? And a *ghost* who went running off without permission?"

Miranda's heart thumped. Perfume?

"Answer me, young lady."

Miranda could only shake her head. Helen grabbed Miranda's arm and propelled her out of the room. Then she half pushed, half dragged her up the stairs. The magnolia scent was even more intense on the second floor. They stopped at the foot of the attic stairs. "Get up there!" Helen shoved Miranda at the steps so viciously that Miranda fell to her knees. "I said, get up there!" Miranda moved slowly up the stairs, her shins aching from the fall.

"It's a pity the latch is broken." Helen tried to force the lock back into place. "But you will remain up here just the same. You are not to come down until your father gets home and I discuss with him what is to be done with you."

Miranda jerked herself free and glared at her mother, trying hard to hold back the tears that coursed down her cheeks. "You're crazy!" she screamed. "And Dad will think so, too, when he hears!"

She edged backward as Helen advanced in fury. She crouched in the corner by the low bookcases under the windows, and Helen towered over her. Miranda cried out with fear, for the cold eyes that glittered at her from her mother's face were Lucinda's own.

Miranda remained crouched in the corner for a long time after Helen had left the attic. Despite the closeness of the oppressive heat, she was cold. Her bruised shins ached from the fall on the stairs. She circled her legs with her arms and rested her chin on her knees.

"That was like my dream," she whispered to herself. "My mother wasn't my mother." Tears began pouring down her cheeks and she wiped them away impatiently.

The sun had disappeared behind a cloud and the attic was steeped in gloom. Miranda didn't dare go out to the landing to turn on the overhead bulb; what if her mother still lurked there, waiting? No, not her mother. *Lucinda*.

Behind the dollhouse she arranged the pillows and sank down onto them. Had it been Lucinda looking out from Iris Kramer's eyes that afternoon when she locked the boys in the attic? Miranda rubbed her own eyes. Nothing made sense. Aunt Belle said it was the house. Had Lucinda's mad eyes glittered on the porch that night, too? Miranda shook her head as if to clear it. The thoughts tumbled through her mind in unordered fury, leaving her exhausted.

She wanted her father. She wanted Dan. She wanted Mrs. Wainwright—anyone to help her out of this nightmare. More than anyone, she wanted her mother. Her own, real Mither. Yet she was alone. But no, not alone—the dollhouse seemed to glow softly as Miranda turned to it. On her knees, she stared through the dollhouse attic windows.

Dorothy pounded small fists on the door. Her petticoat hung limply around her thin frame, and her once shiny curls were in tangles around her face. She had dragged an old blanket out of one of the steamer trunks and wrapped it tightly around herself for warmth. Snow lay on the windowsill outside.

"Mama, Mama! Please come!" she wailed, but her hoarse little voice barely carried across the attic. "Daddy!" she sobbed. "I'm sorry! I'll never be bad again. Please let me out! I'm so cold!"

Miranda started to cry again, aching for the child whose mother was already dead and whose father was only across the street at the Hootons'. Poor Sigmund, grief-stricken, believing he had lost both wife and daughter in the wreck; how much more terrible it would have been for him to know that little Dorothy died of thirst and cold while he himself was soothed and comforted by his neighbors.

Miranda turned away, her tears dropping onto her cheeks. The attic room that had seemed such a haven to her lately now felt evil, angry. The black hole leading down to the secret chamber yawned at her from across the room. She trembled, resolutely tearing her eyes away again. Don't think of that. She turned back to the dollhouse.

Dorothy lay on the floor near the bookcases shivering under her blanket. Long gaspy breaths rasped from her parched throat. How many days had she been in the attic now? How long could a little girl survive without food or water or warmth?

Dorothy's hand inched out across the floorboards and loosely covered an object. The hand closed weakly around it and brought it to her side. A crayon, Miranda could see. A thick, black crayon.

The child dragged her body across the floor to the window and tried to open the sash. It slid a few inches, and she edged out a hand to bring in some more snow to eat, but the snow that had been keeping her alive had melted. Her hand dropped back inside, and she crept over toward Miranda and the dollhouse.

"You poor baby," wept Miranda, feeling somewhat crazed herself at not being able to help. "What can I do? There must be something I can do!"

Dorothy leaned her hand feebly on the dollhouse, and Miranda saw her clearly through the windows. Her blue eyes were filmy and wild-looking. Her mouth hung limp, lips cracked and bleeding. Dorothy dragged herself around the back of the dollhouse and disappeared from view.

"Now she's just where I'm sitting," thought Miranda. "What in the world can she be doing? She's too far gone to play—"

Dorothy came into view again and let the black crayon clatter to the floor, where it rolled under the bookcase. She stared fixedly at the dollhouse, stared directly through the attic windows, and for a split second Miranda's eyes met hers. Dorothy let out a tortured, choked sound and backed away in fright.

"She's seen me!" cried Miranda in wonderment. "She's seen me!"

Dorothy staggered backwards across the attic until she hit the far wall, then seemed to gather the remnants of her strength and knelt to pry open the heavy trapdoor. She propped it up with a small piece of wood, then seemed to lose her balance and fell straight into the hole. Her foot knocked the wooden brace as she fell, and the trapdoor slammed shut. There was no sound in the attic.

Miranda closed her eyes. "No, no, no!" Dorothy had fallen into what would become her grave, and Miranda was powerless to help her.

Did Dorothy hope the secret room would hide her from the face she had seen in the dollhouse? Had her fear of Miranda sent her to her death? Miranda clenched her fists. So it was not as she and Dan had figured. Dorothy had not smothered while playing Underground Railroad—nor had Lucinda murdered her and hidden her in the room. By some bizarre twist of reality, Miranda herself had sent Dorothy fleeing into the airtight chamber.

"She fell in because of me!" The realization ripped through Miranda's head, sending waves of nausea into the pit of her stomach. "Dan and I got it wrong. We never realized how horrible it really was." She sank back onto the cushions and closed her eyes. She felt utterly sick.

Maybe she slept. Or maybe her mind had grown numb from the shock; but Miranda sat up some time later feeling groggy. Her stomach rumbled. The sky outside the attic windows was growing dark.

Something made her turn back to the dollhouse. Lucinda sat at the vanity table in the master bedroom, smoothing her delicately arched brows and pinking her cheeks with soft color. She fluffed back her shiny hair and smiled into the mirror. "Hello, beauty," she murmured to her reflection.

"You witch," wept Miranda. "Little Snow White is dead now, and you didn't even need a poisoned apple!" She watched Lucinda apply the magnolia-scented perfume to her long, slender neck, and the thought struck her that this wicked queen had not lived even as long as Dorothy that day. She tried to feel sorry about that and failed.

"Mama? Can I come with you?"

"Your grammar, Dorothy. You'll never get ahead in life if you don't speak properly."

"*May* I come with you? Please?" There was Dorothy again, sweet in her flouncy lace petticoat, dimpling at her mother in an attempt at persuasion.

It was like watching the rerun of a horror movie. Miranda already knew the end, yet she felt compelled to watch again as Dorothy was spanked with the hairbrush for spilling the magnolia perfume and dragged up to the attic. Miranda winced, her slapped face and bruised shins a stinging reminder of her own mother's assault. Lucinda locked the door and slipped the key into the pocket of her gown.

She returned to the vanity and began pinning up her hair. Finally, after a last satisfactory inspection in the mirror, she started downstairs, calling up the attic steps to Dorothy: "I want you quiet up there, young lady. An afternoon in the cold will teach you to mind your mother!" She sailed off downstairs.

Miranda caught the scent of burning bread early this time and waited impatiently at the kitchen window, watching Donald and staring at the calendar on the wall until Lucinda hurried into the room. January 1904. The sleigh scene. "Sigmund to New York" on the 19th.

"Damnation!" cried Lucinda, jerking off her coat and swishing her gown angrily. The *pinging* noise sounded sharply as Lucinda dropped her coat onto a chair and hurried to draw the charred loaves from the oven. Miranda fastened her attention on the sound. This time the insignificant little noise rang with importance. How could she have missed it before?

Something had dropped to the floor. But what?

Something Lucinda was carrying—or something that fell out of . . . a pocket. Out of her coat pocket when she threw it on the chair—a coin, perhaps? Or out of her dress pocket when she angrily swished her skirt at the delay—could it be the *key?*

Miranda stared into the kitchen long after Lucinda and Donald departed, laughing, into the snow. The floor under the chair was bare. Yet Lucinda had not picked up whatever it was she had dropped. The thing, whatever it was, must have fallen between the floorboards.

# 22

A plan began to form at the back of Miranda's mind. She ran to the attic door, opening it quietly. She steeled herself to meet her mother. Dorothy's life was at stake. She crept down the stairs, hugging the walls to avoid the creaking steps.

At the foot of the stairs, she stopped to listen. The door to her parents' room was closed. A radio played faintly. She hoped the radio would cover any sounds she made. She hung on to the banister as she tiptoed down to the first floor. Still, the last step squeaked, and she waited motionless in the front hall, poised to run.

But the house was still, except for the soft music from the radio. Miranda glided soundlessly across the dim hallway, through the dining room, and to the kitchen. So far, so good.

She scooped a flashlight off the pantry shelf and switched it on, then tried to orient herself. There were the windows she looked through when at the doll-house. The iron stove had stood there in the corner; the calendar had hung on that wall above the breakfast table. And the chair where Lucinda had thrown her fur coat had stood . . . here. Miranda crossed the room and knelt on the floor, sucking in her breath. She had forgotten the stained linoleum. That stupid Iris Kramer! Why had she bothered modernizing the kitchen? The wide floorboards of the Galworthys' kitchen must lie under the yellowed sheet of linoleum. Miranda scanned the room. What could she use as a tool to pry the linoleum up?

Just then the hall light blazed, scattering the shadows. She could hear Helen's footsteps coming down the stairs. Miranda stood stock still, looking around wildly for an escape route.

The cellar! She opened the door just enough to squeeze through and, turning off her flashlight, scuttled down the cement steps into darkness. The cellar was cool, but too quiet. She couldn't hear what was going on in the rest of the house. Was her mother in the kitchen? There was no way to tell. She crouched under the stairs, biting the inside of her cheek when something crawled over her bare arm in the dark.

She sat there rubbing her bruised shins, waiting for what seemed like hours but was, according to the lighted face of her wristwatch, only fifteen minutes. Then she crept back up the cellar steps and opened the door a crack. The kitchen was empty, and no light shone in from the hall. The coast was clear; now to get that linoleum up.

Working in the glow of the flashlight, she used a kitchen knife as a combination saw and lever, digging it into the cracked floor covering. Eventually a torn edge loosened, and she grabbed hold of it with her fingers and pulled with all her might. The sound of the old glue ripping away from the floorboards beneath tore through the quiet kitchen. She froze, poised to leap back down the cellar steps at the first sound from the rooms beyond. She felt as if she were trapped with a dangerous stranger.

When no sound came, Miranda inched her fingers along the floorboards beneath the linoleum. There was a deep crevice between the wide boards. She held her flashlight over the crack, hoping to catch the gleam of silver in its light. She could see nothing.

"Damnation!" The syllables hung in the air as they had when Lucinda shrieked them almost a century ago in that very room. But this time *Miranda* had uttered the expletive. She was certain the key had fallen here. Could someone else have found it already? When Iris Kramer remodeled the kitchen, had the key been found by workmen? But who would look down into cracks in the floor unless they knew something had been lost there?

In angry desperation, Miranda ripped back another section of linoleum, revealing two more wide floor-boards. She stabbed her knife deep into the cracks. She had been so sure she was on the right track — but there was nothing.

She pulled back more of the floor covering, her breath coming in short sobs. This time her knife met with resistance, and she twisted it sideways to scoop out whatever blocked the blade. Slowly she levered out of the crack a small round disk. She could have broken down in tears right then and there when she saw it was only a coin, but her sense of urgency was too great. She couldn't afford the time a good cry would take. She rubbed the coin on her shorts, and as the grease and grime changed surfaces, she saw she held a quarter. She squinted to make out the date: 1898. It might have fallen into the crack years before Lucinda dropped the attic key. Or maybe Lucinda had dropped a coin that day—not a key, after all!

Miranda leaned back on her hands and closed her eyes, straining to remember every detail of the scene she had watched. Lucinda threw her coat down and swirled her skirt. The key must have landed under the chair she was standing beside. But what if it bounced and landed somewhere else? What if it had been found decades ago and thrown away as worthless?

There was only one crack left to check. Miranda bit her lip. She felt the sweat running down under her thin T-shirt and the throb of the darkening bruises on her shins as she worked to scrape through the old dirt.

Then she heard it at last—the beautiful scraping sound of metal touching metal.

"Careful," she cautioned herself. "It could be just another coin." But she dug frantically, just the same.

And at last, there it was, retrieved from its narrow grave after so many years: a large, tarnished key. Clenching it in her fist, Miranda threw both arms high in a victory V.

She stowed the key safely in her pocket, then set about pressing the stained linoleum sheet back into place. She couldn't imagine what her parents would say when they noticed it had been pulled up. She placed a kitchen chair over the mutilated section, laid the knife in the sink, and turned off her flashlight. Now to get back to the attic without being seen.

Just as she began sidling up the stairs to the second floor, her parents' bedroom door opened and Helen crossed the hall to the bathroom. The door closed. Over the pounding in her head, Miranda heard the sound of running water. She tiptoed up a few more steps, then froze as car headlights swept into the driveway, their beam penetrating like a searchlight through the front door screen. Her father was home — thank God!

She raced up the stairs now, hardly caring if they creaked. She had to get up to the attic — and fast. Dorothy was waiting. Dorothy was counting on her.

At the top of the attic stairs the old rush of terror hit her. Her throat grew parched; her lips felt thick and dry. The timeless refrain roared through her head: *Helpmehelpmehelpme! I'm going to die, going to die!*

*Not if I can help it!* thought Miranda. The scent of magnolia was very strong, the terror so acute that she nearly turned and fled. But she wrapped her arms around herself resolutely and crossed to the dollhouse. She knelt behind it and looked through the little attic windows.

Dorothy dropped the black crayon and staggered backward.

"No!" whispered Miranda, turning away. "No! That's

too late." She looked back again. This time she saw Timmy Kramer crouching over the small fire in the corner.

"Hey, come here, Timmy!" Jeff called. "Look at this little crack — "

"No!" cried Miranda, closing her eyes as the flames suddenly leapt from the corner to the wall by the trapdoor. "Dorothy, where are you?"

She heard voices conferring below her on the second floor. What lies was Lucinda telling her father? In desperation, Miranda turned back to the dollhouse. This time through the windows she saw an empty attic. Toys filled the white bookcase under the windows. Snow filtered down outside. It was Dorothy's attic playroom!

Footsteps clattered up the wooden stairs and Miranda held her breath. Were her own parents coming up, or was it — ?

The door burst open, and regal Lucinda stormed in on a wave of magnolia perfume. She dragged Dorothy by the arm. Dorothy fell to the floor as her mother yanked her into the room. "Don't hurt me, Mama!"

"I've had it, you little brat." Lucinda's voice was cold and her eyes glittered. "Any more nonsense out of you, and you'll get it again."

She stepped away, smoothing her hands over her gown. "Dorothy, you will stay up here until your father gets home. You will stay up here until you can learn deportment. I will not have a clumsy, willful, disobedient child in this house." With these words she turned

and exited, locking the door. Soon Donald would arrive and she would leave forever.

Dorothy raced to the door. "Mama!" she cried,
kicking the door with her small, bare feet. "Let me
out, Mama!"

Miranda hunched over the dollhouse, waiting, not
daring to look away from the attic scene. She waited
while Dorothy sobbed and pleaded, waited until Lucinda finished getting ready and called up the stairs:
"I want you quiet up there, young lady. An afternoon
in the cold will teach you to mind your mother!" She
waited until she was positive that Lucinda and Donald
had left the house.

"She'll have dropped the key," whispered Miranda.
"But *I've* got it now!"

Dorothy stopped crying and sat shivering beside
her bookcase of toys. She pulled a blanket out of an
open trunk, wrapped it around herself, and settled
down to play with a puzzle and wait for her father.
After a while she started humming to herself and
picked up her little dolls. She carried them over to the
dollhouse.

Miranda held her breath as Dorothy disappeared
from view behind the house. Then she pulled the
tarnished key from her pocket and set it in the dollhouse attic.

The childish singing broke off with an exclamation
of surprise, and Dorothy emerged from Miranda's
corner, trailing the blanket. She held the now bright
and shiny key in one hand, a puzzled expression on
her face.

The dollhouse had worked the magic. Miranda stared at the space where the tarnished key had been in the dollhouse attic only seconds before, and let out her breath. "Go on!" she urged Dorothy aloud. "Don't just stand here wondering how the key got there! Take it and get out of the attic! Go over to the Hootons'— go anywhere! Just go!"

Dorothy hesitated at the door, staring down at the key in her small hand. A hundred questions must have been tumbling through her mind. Her eyes swept the room and stopped at the dollhouse.

Miranda stared hard at Dorothy through the windows. "I can't do any more," she yelled. "Now you have to save yourself!"

Dorothy's eyes widened with something like fear. She pressed her hands to her mouth. Her eyes met Miranda's and the expression changed for a second, becoming old and very wise. "Thank you, Dollhouse," she said in her soft, childish voice. Then she turned away and, with a strange sound—half cry, half laugh— unlocked the door and fled from the attic.

# 23

"Oh, there you are, Mandy," said Helen as Miranda slowly emerged from the attic. Miranda shrank against the wall.

"What is it?" cried Helen, running to her. "You look—funny. Do you feel all right? Have you been up there all afternoon?"

Miranda shook her head. "I'm going to bed," she whispered, staring past her mother into the hall. It looked different, somehow. Or was it only that the earlier atmosphere of menace was gone?

"Don't you want some dinner? We've just ordered out for pizza."

"Is Dad home?" The atmosphere *was* different. Lighter, airy. Less stifling, as if the weather had changed while she was up in the attic, and strong winds had blown away the humidity.

"He's down in the kitchen." Helen placed a gentle hand on Miranda's forehead. "You don't feel feverish. But it must be awfully hot in the attic. Why don't you take a bath and get into bed? I'll bring you up some pizza." She stroked Miranda's hair. "Tomato with extra cheese. How does that sound?"

"Fine," croaked Miranda, and she disappeared to soak in the tub.

She lay in the bath full of bubbles, eyes closed, relief washing over her with the warm water. She knew she was safe. And Dorothy was safe. That was all that mattered now. She was too tired to wash. She simply rested, watching the fluffy bubbles grow thin. When they had melted away to a film on top of the water and she stood up to get out, she gasped. She touched her legs gently with probing fingers and felt no pain at all. The bruises on her shins were gone.

She mulled things over in bed with her pizza. If Dorothy had escaped from the attic, she didn't die in the secret room after all. That meant, of course, that her body couldn't have been found there.

But how could that be? Could that possibly be true? She scarcely dared to think so. Could time change, just like that? As quickly as a snap of fingers in the air? As quickly as a key could turn in a lock?

Philip walked by in the hall. "Dad!" she called.

"Hi." He stuck his head into the room. "Are you feeling better?"

"Sort of," she said, breathlessly. "Come here a second, will you?"

He walked over to her bed. "Not deathly contagious, I trust?"

"No," she said. "Dad? Where's the newspaper?"

"Today's? Downstairs, I think. I thought you read it at breakfast."

"Not today's. The day before yesterday's."

"It's probably in the pile for recycling."

She tried to smile at him. "Would you mind bringing it up to me? I want to read something again."

He raised his brows at her, but went downstairs and returned a few moments later with the *Garnet Star.* "Here you go. Nothing very exciting, I'm afraid."

"No?" Miranda grabbed the paper and scanned the front page. The headlines that had screamed the discovery of the mummified body now announced a demonstration against nuclear weapons in Washington and a political meeting in Egypt. A bank had been robbed in Boston, and two Garnet teenagers had been caught trying to steal bicycles in the park. She double-checked the date. It was the right one, but there was nothing at all about a dead child in Miranda's attic.

She stretched out under the sheet and let the paper drop to the floor. She lifted the cover and stared down at her body, double-checking her legs. There were no bruises — somehow it was true! Dorothy was saved — the past was changed, and so was the present. She couldn't even begin to think what this might mean. Her mind refused to ponder the imponderable. She lay back in bed, utterly exhausted, and slept without stirring until morning.

Birds in the tree outside the window woke her. She lay still for a few minutes, all senses alert. Then she slid out of bed and cautiously moved across the room to pull some clean clothes from her dresser. She moved gingerly, feeling the newness of everything, the freshness of the air. She walked down the steps, testing each tread with her foot before putting her weight on it. It seemed anything could happen.

She ate cereal at the breakfast table while Philip sipped his diet shake. Surreptitiously she stole a glance at the floor and felt dizzy when she saw the old, worn linoleum was smooth, untorn. It had never been touched.

"Are you feeling better this morning, Mandy?" asked Helen.

"Yes," she nodded, taking a muffin from the plate Helen set on the table. She noticed a whole row of small containers filled with soil lined up on the windowsill over the sink. Small leafy plants poked through the dirt. In one pot Miranda recognized mint leaves; in another, chives. But her mother had spent so much time lying in bed with headaches, she hadn't had time to start the herb garden she wanted. At least, the windowsill had been empty yesterday. Where had these herbs come from?"

"Ed and I need to go back to Lexington this morning," said Philip. "It's fascinating work, the museum business. Helen, do you know—I may have found a new vocation!"

"That's great, Phil!"

"Do you want to come along, Mandy?"

"Not really. Thanks, though." Her voice was soft. She couldn't seem to reach normal volume.

Helen smiled. "Don't you and Dan have plans for a picnic today?" She slipped a fried egg onto Philip's plate.

"Umm —," said Miranda vaguely.

"Take it away, Helen. I've had my egg for the week already."

"Oops! Sorry." She nudged it back onto the spatula. "Mandy?"

"Okay." She picked up her fork and stabbed the yolk.

Philip poured Helen some coffee, then emptied the rest of the pot into his own cup. He rattled the newspaper. "Look, there's another good film in town this week. Shall we go see it?"

"Sure, why not? This seems to be our summer for movies." They started talking about all the good ones they'd seen so far. Miranda picked at her muffin. As far as she knew, no one had gone out to a movie since they'd left New York. Miranda felt a stab of fear in her stomach and pushed away her plate.

"Look, are you still thinking about moving?" she interrupted their conversation.

Helen stared at her, and Philip lowered his coffee mug. "Moving?" he asked.

"Is something the matter? Don't you like it here, Mandy?" asked Helen. "You seem to be enjoying yourself —"

"Oh, I am. I do." Miranda assured her. "But I just thought *you* wanted to move. You know, because you don't like the house."

"Why would I not like the house?" asked Helen. She looked confused. "We've only been here a month! I thought we all agreed it's the greatest place in the world!"

"Never mind," said Miranda. She carried her plate and cup to the sink. "Well, I'm going for a bike ride with Dan."

"Have fun. But, honey? Be sure to come in and lie down if you start feeling sick again." Helen began to clear the table.

Philip carried his mug to the sink. "Oh, Mandy, don't forget you have that extra flute lesson this afternoon. Mrs. Wainwright called this morning and said you'd arranged it with her the other day. I guess you're anxious to be in top form for the autumn concert."

"Umm, yeah," murmured Miranda. She was out the door before either of them could ask again if she was feeling all right. As far as she knew, she had never arranged a special lesson.

Miranda rode across the street and waited on the Hootons' front porch until Dan bounded out. "Dad said you should come in for coffee cake," he said, "but I told him we wanted to get going. I had a hard time keeping Buddy from coming along, too, until I told him where we were going. He always freaks in graveyards."

"The graveyard? I thought we'd decided to stay away from there."

He looked surprised. "I thought the whole point was that you wanted to see it!"

Miranda shrugged. "Let's go then."

They rode side by side up the hill. "I have to talk to you," began Miranda, pumping hard to keep pace.

"I have to talk to you, too," he answered sternly.

"Will you or will you not come with us to Cape Cod next week? What did your parents say? I'm dying of suspense!"

Miranda didn't answer. Cape Cod? What was he talking about? She felt a stab of fear again. She cleared her throat and rode behind him as a car passed. "I have to talk to you, first," she called.

"About what?"

"Well, about the secret room, to start with."

"Yours or ours?"

"Mine." So at least he knew they had found one. "Listen, Dan. There *wasn't* a dead body in it. The paper said so!"

"What!" Dan braked with a screech of tires and she nearly crashed her bike into his. "The newspaper said 'No dead body was found in Miranda Browne's attic'?"

"Of course not, idiot. It didn't mention a body at all. That's what I mean. You know if we'd found a body, they would have reported it."

Dan stared at her in astonishment. "I guess I have to agree with you there. But since there wasn't any body, why should you be surprised that the papers didn't report it?"

Miranda bit her lip. "Dan? You're going to think I'm weird, but — "

"Correction! I *already* think you're weird."

She pressed on. "Just answer me, okay? Did we find a body of a dead girl in my attic? Or not?"

Dan laughed shortly and mounted his bike again. "Of course we did, poor thing. We found bodies all over the house. My house, too. Blood and guts. We'll see more at the graveyard, if you want." He shook his head and pedaled ahead of her, yelling back over his shoulder: "What's the matter with you today?"

Miranda gritted her teeth and pumped hard.

The cornfields gave way to the old graveyard on their right. They turned into the gravel drive, stopping in a grove of trees just outside the stone wall. They dismounted and wandered in.

"It's great that you're interested in old stones, too," said Dan. "Do you know how to take charcoal rubbings? I'll have to show you sometime. You just need a big sheet of paper and a piece of charcoal or a crayon. You tape the paper to a gravestone and rub the charcoal over it—and you get a perfect copy of the inscription and carvings!"

Miranda's mind was not on charcoal rubbings. She led Dan to the leaning stones of the older graves and stopped in front of one. "Look there!" she breathed.

In Loving Memory
LUCINDA WALKER GALWORTHY
Nov 1873–Jan 1904
Beloved Wife of Sigmund Galworthy
Cherished Mother of Dorothy
"THE LORD GIVETH AND THE LORD TAKETH AWAY"

"What's wrong?" asked Dan in alarm.

"It doesn't say that Dorothy's dead, too!" She ran to check the nearby stones. "See? Her grave isn't here at all!"

"Dorothy *who?*" he shouted.

Miranda burst into tears. "You really don't remember?" she cried. "Don't you remember anything about Dorothy and the dollhouse?"

Dan looked worried. "Come on, Mandy. Let's get out of here." He shook his head. "Come on, don't cry. I think we should go home."

Miranda hurled herself away from him. It was too much. He was staring at her as if she were not quite sane.

"Do you want to tell me what's wrong?" Dan asked gently. "Sometimes if you talk about what's bothering you, it helps."

Miranda took a deep breath and leaned against a fallen gravestone. Dan might not remember, but he had been the one who warned her: changing the past means changing the present, too. She needed him to remember — but maybe she would just have to consider herself lucky. The present could have become even *more* changed. What if saving Dorothy had meant that somehow the Brownes never moved to Garnet in the first place? What if it meant that so many little things were different because Dorothy hadn't died in the attic that the present was wholly unrecognizable? Dorothy's life might have influenced the world in such a way that, somehow, Miranda herself would never have been born! Things could be worse, she told herself.

Dan crouched beside her now. She stared into his eyes for a moment, then reached for his hands — the same warm hands she had held when they tried to summon Dorothy.

"All right," she said in a choked voice. "I'm going to tell you a story. Just promise you won't interrupt until I'm finished."

He nodded. She released his hands, then picked a blade of grass and stared at it. "It all began when we moved to Garnet and I went up to the attic and found the dollhouse a fugitive slave once built . . ."

Dan lay back and stared up at the sky, appearing to fall asleep as her voice droned on. Miranda carefully related the tale and his own part in it.

"And then after we found the body, I started thinking maybe Dorothy was somehow letting me see through the dollhouse windows because she wanted help. We tried to contact her to find out how we could help her to rest in peace." Miranda was dry-mouthed after more than a half hour of uninterrupted speaking. "But then you gave me the idea of altering the past. You pointed out that changing the past would change the present—and it kind of hit me that what Dorothy really wanted was for me to change things so that she didn't die in the attic at all! And that sure was something I wanted to do for her—it was so horrible, you know, seeing her fall into that hole right before my eyes. Anyway, eventually I figured out where to find the key. I put it in the dollhouse attic, and Dorothy found it there and let herself out. She was saved!" Miranda clenched a handful of grass, ripping it out of the ground. "Okay? The end."

Dan reached out and pulled her over on the grass next to him. "It sounds as if—," he began slowly, "—as if you really believe all this happened."

"It *did* happen, Dan!"

He leaned back on his arms and stared up at the sky, dark brows drawn together. "Let me make sure I get this. You are actually asking me to believe that you and I spent time doing all sorts of things this past week or so—even though I have no memory of them?"

"You got it," she said.

"Doesn't that sound pretty bizarre—even to you?" Now he was scowling. "I mean, look. What if I came over to your house and said, 'Oh, Mandy, don't you remember how we flew to Mars last week in this totally amazing spaceship piloted by beings with three heads? You don't? Well, that must be because they zapped you with a laser beam to make you forget it ever happened. But, lucky me, I remember everything.'" He glared at her.

"Oh—never mind, Dan!"

"Yeah. Would you believe a story like that?"

"Probably not," she admitted. "But, I swear to you—everything I said is true."

"Magic Mandy the Mystic Oracle," he said mildly enough, but she couldn't bear it. She started to cry again. All the tight control of the past weeks, all the tension she'd carried with her from her parents' quarrels, all the stress of unshed tears and unexpressed terror poured out now. She turned and rested her forehead against Lucinda's gravestone, pressing her fist into her mouth to stifle the sobs.

She pushed Dan away when he tried to embrace her. "Just leave me alone! Forget it!"

"Oh, Mandy!" He wrapped her in his arms, ignoring her struggles. "I'm sorry! I really am—it's just that I don't know what I'm supposed to do!"

She finally rested her head against his chest. "I guess there isn't anything you can do. I just feel so alone!"

He ran his fingers through her hair. They were silent for several minutes while he twirled one of her curls around his finger. "You're a fantastic storyteller, that's for sure. You make me *want* to believe it!"

She shrugged and picked at the grass. "I could never make up something like this."

"Hmm. But—how did the magic work? How did you know Dorothy would be able to get the key out of the dollhouse?"

"I didn't know. But when you said yesterday that death is always a mistake, it got me thinking that maybe Dorothy was trying to tell me that she didn't want to rest in peace at all. I thought, well, how could she get out of the attic before she fell into the hole? And when I heard the key fall from Lucinda's pocket, I thought of trying to find it again. The dollhouse was sort of a time machine—it was the only place I could put the key that connected *then* with *now*."

She fell silent. Then a thought struck her. "You know, maybe it wasn't Dorothy's spirit after all. Maybe it was Lucinda's—there was always that perfume. Maybe she felt guilty all these years and wanted someone to undo the damage she'd caused. Oh, I don't know!" She rubbed her head. "It gives me a headache to think about it. And, you know? I saw that scene when Lucinda dropped the key several times before I even thought about what it could mean! I can't believe I was so stupid."

"Wouldn't your parents have helped you? Didn't you tell them about the dollhouse?"

"I didn't — it seemed like the dollhouse didn't want me to." She remembered the lure she'd felt pulling her up to the attic. "I had the feeling it was *my* secret. Like no one else was supposed to know about the magic."

"So how come you ended up telling me about it?"

She smiled at him faintly. "You bullied me into it."

"That's about the first thing you've said that I can believe!"

Her smile faded.

"Look," he said, "I just wish you could show me some proof."

"I know, I know," she responded irritably. "That's what you kept saying before."

"Before — ," he murmured and fell silent.

They lay there listening to the birds chirping. Miranda let her mind drift back to the first time she'd come to this graveyard and found Dorothy's grave: how she and Dan had tried to summon Dorothy; how the air and grass and fields around them all seemed to come alive. "Life," she murmured. "That's what Dorothy was trying to tell us."

She tipped her face up to the sun and let the other memories come — all the memories of her life since she had moved to Garnet and discovered the dollhouse. There were funny, shadowy areas, she discovered. Times she was not so certain about anymore. A hazy sort of feeling, with some new memories taking shape in the fog. Memories of picnics with Dan, visiting museums in Lexington and Concord with her father and Ed Hooton, helping her mother decorate the new office in town, making plans to visit the Hootons' summer house on Cape Cod—memories of events that had never happened, or had not happened until she altered time. Yet those foggy memories grew clearer every moment, and the dollhouse began to seem as remote and elusive as something she once dreamed. The old graveyard had never been so peaceful.

"I *didn't* make it up, Dan," she said softly. "But there's no way to prove it. It's all over now, anyway."

"Why is it over? What do you mean?"

"Don't you get it?" Miranda spit out a blade of grass and looked at him earnestly. "Because of Dorothy. If I altered time, then Dorothy never died in the attic, and we never found her body. Even if it were Lucinda haunting the attic, it works the same way. If Dorothy didn't die there, then Lucinda didn't need to feel guilty for killing her. It never happened! Dorothy escaped that day and left the house—she probably went over to your house, and her father found her there when he came home! She didn't die in the attic, so she didn't need to be saved. The magic dollhouse couldn't have happened."

Dan twirled a buttercup under her chin. "Hmm. Sounds like you need a course in logic when school starts."

She pushed the flower away. "Well, if there's one thing I've learned, it's that logic isn't everything."

"There are so many things I don't understand, Mandy. Things no one understands, I guess. Time is one of them." He looked at her seriously. "Like we see only the tip of the iceberg."

"Yes," she agreed emphatically.

A gentle breeze drifted over the cornfields and stirred the grass near the gravestones. "Still," said Dan, "if it happened, it isn't fair I can't remember!"

"I wish you could remember, too," she told him. "It would make the whole thing seem less of a dream."

"The way you tell it makes me feel the story is almost a memory of mine." He took her hand and examined her palm. "And you're *positive* it wasn't a dream?"

She smiled at him, quite positive. And she realized it didn't matter if he ever believed her. Dorothy had lived; *that* was what counted.

Dan squeezed her fingers in his. "And your mother doesn't remember, either?"

"It doesn't look like it. God, yesterday I was so scared of her — I thought I hated her — but it wasn't really Mither at all. Lucinda was hanging around all this time, and I never realized it." She shivered, remembering those cold, glittering eyes.

"So you're the *only* one who remembers anything?"

Miranda hesitated, recalling the startled, wise expression in Dorothy's eyes as she met Miranda's through the dollhouse windows. "I'm not sure," she said slowly. "I think Dorothy knew for a second."

Back at the house, Miranda climbed the stairs to the attic again, and knelt on the cushions behind the dollhouse. The first thing she noticed when she rested her elbows on the dollhouse attic floor was the absence of the black-crayoned scrawl. Miranda rubbed her fingers over the tiny floorboards where **WATER** had once been written.

"Nothing was ever here," she whispered. "Dorothy left in time."

When she stared through the little windows, she saw only her own ordinary attic. The previously blackened corner of charred wood from the Kramers' fire was now clean and smooth. The fire, too, had never happened. She flopped back onto her pillows. The room was quiet and peaceful, the sense of waiting gone. A gentle breeze filtered in through the open windows.

"Dorothy?" she whispered. "What happened to you?"

But there was no answer.

# Happily . . .

Helen parked the car in front of Mrs. Wainwright's house. Miranda sighed as they climbed the porch steps. If Mrs. Wainwright only knew how busy she had been, she would not expect her to be note-perfect at this specially arranged lesson.

"I'm sorry if I'm late," she began as soon as Mrs. Wainwright opened the front door.

But Mrs. Wainwright brushed aside the apology. "You're not late at all," she said. "I'm afraid *I'm* running over today—but I blame it on my last student. She was the late one."

"Better late than never!" laughed a girl carrying a flute, who appeared in the hallway next to Mrs. Wainwright.

"That's a cliché, Susannah," chided Mrs. Wainwright. "But I suppose it's true, nonetheless." She held the door open for Miranda and Helen. "Well, come in, my dears. Susannah and I were just about to have a glass of iced tea. I need a little break in all this terrible humidity. Oh—I haven't introduced you! Susannah

Johnston, Helen and Miranda Browne. Helen is a doctor, Susannah dear. So you'll have to talk to her." She turned to Helen. "I've been trying to make a musician out of Susannah, but she is determined to be a doctor!"

"And the music world will rejoice," said Susannah dryly.

"Nonsense!" said Mrs. Wainwright. "You just need to — "

"Practice!" chimed Miranda and Susannah together. They looked at each other and laughed.

"You girls will be in eighth grade this year, won't you?" asked Mrs. Wainwright.

Both girls nodded.

"And Miranda lives in the old Galworthy House now, so you two have something else in common." Just then the phone rang, and Mrs. Wainwright hurried to the living room. "I won't be long," she called back over her shoulder. "Why don't you all go pour yourselves some tea?"

Miranda led the way into the kitchen. They sat down at the kitchen table.

"Have you been taking lessons long?" asked Helen.

"Only about forever," sighed Susannah. "It was my great-grandmother's idea in the first place, but she and Mrs. Wainwright are old friends, so they're in it together now. Determined to wring music out of a rock. My great-grandmother thinks young ladies should have certain accomplishments. Like music, you know. And sewing."

"Can you sew?" asked Miranda.

"Not a stitch." Susannah grinned and stuck a wad of gum in her mouth. "I'm telling you, it's my great-grandmother's big despair in life that I'm not accomplished."

"Oh, well," said Miranda. "Maybe you can take a basic home ec class in school."

"I'll be too busy tackling chemistry and physics!"

Helen laughed. "Good for you!"

"So when did you move here?" asked Susannah, tossing her long blonde curls over her shoulder.

"About a month ago, but it seems longer," answered Miranda, looking at Susannah's hair. "From New York."

"I've always wanted to live in a big city," said Susannah eagerly.

"Oh, no! I think Garnet is much nicer!"

Susannah shrugged. "My family has lived here for a million years. I'd like to go someplace new." She poured herself some iced tea and handed the pitcher to Miranda.

Miranda set it aside. "Why did Mrs. Wainwright say we have something in common — besides being in the same grade, I mean?"

"You both play the flute," Helen pointed out.

"True," said Susannah. "But she meant because my great-grandmother lived in your house when she was little."

Miranda's heart skipped a beat. "Your — grandmother?" she whispered.

Susannah looked at her curiously over the rim of her glass. "*Great*-grandmother. The one I was telling you about, who wants me to sew and be a musical prodigy and stuff. Her ancestors built the house, and she was born there. The family's name was Galworthy; that's why people still call it the Galworthy House, even though lots of other people have lived in it since then. I think it's listed that way on the *Register of Historic Houses*."

"Oh, how interesting!" said Helen.

"Why doesn't your family still live in it?" was all Miranda could get out, although a hundred questions tumbled through her mind.

"Well, when Nonny—that's what I call her—when she was a little girl, her mother was killed in a train wreck. Her father was really devastated, and they moved out of town to Boston. But when she got older, Nonny came back to Garnet to teach school, and she married Pop."

"Who was it—the guy she married?"

"My great-grandfather!" laughed Susannah, not understanding Miranda's interest.

"But what was his *name?*" she pressed urgently. Helen glanced at her curiously.

But Susannah answered with a smile. "His name *is* Joseph Johnston. They live on Greenapple Lane, just past the high school. They're both really old—in their nineties, can you believe it? Nonny still gets around really well—still drives, and everything—but Pop is in a wheelchair now. They were childhood sweethearts. Isn't that romantic?" Susannah lifted her hair off her shoulders, then let it drop again. "God, it's hot!"

Miranda twisted a paper napkin. She felt like crying, like laughing, like singing. She felt she had found a long-lost friend. Dorothy!

Dorothy had lived, had grown up and taught school, had married the neighbor boy who liked her so much — Joey Johnston — and had a child! Miranda stared at Susannah Johnston with wide eyes. She knew where she'd seen hair like that before. Here was the living proof. Dorothy's great-granddaughter!

Mrs. Wainwright bustled into the kitchen, her bright-colored scarves floating out behind her. "I'm sorry I was so long," she apologized. "Come, Miranda, let's go right on to your lesson."

"Hey, how about if I wait till you're finished," Susannah suggested. "Then you can meet Nonny! She'll be coming with my mom to pick me up in a few minutes. I know she'll get a kick out of talking to the people who live in her house now."

"We'll sit out on the porch till your lesson's over," said Helen. "It'll be fun to meet her, won't it, Mandy?"

Miranda stood holding her flute, unable to speak. A vision of little Dorothy's tear-stained face and wise old eyes flickered in her head.

"You'll like Nonny," Susannah assured her. "I'm sure you two will have a lot to talk about."

"Yes," murmured Miranda. "Yes, I'm sure we will."

Late afternoon sunlight flooded the music room as Miranda played her flute. Through the light, the music kept rising. The notes soared high and clear, suspended in the summer's day. In the still, warm air her song blended with the timeless smells: fresh cut grass, a hint of rain, and the heavy, sweet scent of magnolia blossoms.